The Colde

MW00945556

A Father Angus MacManus Cozy Mystery

by Larry Finke

Happy Reading!

Larry

What people are saying about

The Coldest Shoulder

I bought it, read two chapters, then gave it to my sister. That'll teach her for stealing my favorite sweater in junior high!
Jennifer Munnings, second cousin

I always knew he had it in him. Unfortunately, he let it out.
Richard Wrye, high school choir director

We'll be taking legal action.
Irene Beethe, American Guild of Organists

As to the publication of this book, let it be known I strongly advised against it.
Father Jon Spinillo, St. Paul's by the Park, Winona, Minnesota

Not bad, not bad, even if he does say so himself.
Terri Brand, Facebook humorist

It kept him out of my hair for over a year, so there's that.
Bonnie Finke, long-suffering wife

My mother always said that if I can't say something nice about someone, I should say nothing at all, so no comment.
Gina Holter, literary critic, Williston North Dakota Herald

As a patient, he wasn't.
Shannon Heeley, nurse

The Coldest Shoulder

A Father Angus MacManus Cozy Mystery

ISBN   978-1-329-14761-4
Imprint: Lulu.com

Acknowledgements
Christopher Finke
Father Jon Spinillo
Jennifer Munnings
Jon Holter
Margaret Claus
Mike Ford
Peytra Traska
Shannon Doberstein
Trina Munnings

Cover by Anna Schroeder-Finke

In memory of
Mark Schweitzer

Thanks for the inspiration

Chapter 1

When Bishop McNally came for his annual visit to the appropriately-named Bicker Harbour, Nova Scotia the third Saturday in February, I was ready to surrender my position as St. Andrew's Episcopal Church's priest. The annual congregational meeting the week prior with its petty squabbles removed any remaining joy in me. I needed to do something drastic for my mental and physical health.

St. Andrew's had its share of ongoing spats – some seemingly going back to the English invasion of 1385 – and I was worn down trying to keep the peace, counsel church members, and maintain worship. The tenure of the last three priests here averaged three years each, and this was my fourth.

My bishop knew St. Andrew's history and also knew I was unhappy. We sat in my rumpled office in two old, brown, threadbare wing-back chairs upholstered in the 1960s. St. Andrew's was nothing if not frugal in that infamous Scottish way.

Bishop McNally looked far younger than his 65 years; I looked older than my 55. He crossed his long, thin legs at the knee, his polished black wingtips gleaming in what evening light came through the grimy office windows. I tucked my short, chubby forelegs and feet under my chair, ashamed in the difference from the bishop's footwear and my sad, shabby chukka boots.

"Angus, I believe you and Mae hold dual citizenship, do you not?" said the Right Reverend. I nodded in agreement. The bishop thought for a minute, coffee mug on his leg containing the cheap brew St. Andrew's provided, and said, "What would you say to dual, ecumenically-minded parishes in the States?"

"I don't know…dual parishes are normally small, but still demand nearly twice the time, what with travel and the necessary administrative work."

"What if I said one was a summer parish and the other a winter?" said the bishop, raising his eyebrows over the rim of his cup, then taking a sip.

"Intriguing. Go on."

"Neither congregation is large in numbers, somewhere between 20 and 50. The summer parish is on a lake island in north-central Minnesota. A bit like Innisfree," he said, referring to the island in a poem by the Irish poet William Butler Yeats:

> *I will arise and go now, and go to Innisfree,*
> *And a small cabin build there, of clay and wattles made:*
> *Nine bean-rows will I have there, a hive for the honey-bee...*

"No cabin made of clay and wattles, and no need to feed yourselves with bean rows. The winter parish is in Texas, made up of some of the same people in the Minnesota parish. Snowbirds and all that. The church building itself in Minnesota was modeled after the ancient priory at Lindisfarne."

Being a history buff and the husband of a history teacher, I was familiar with Lindisfarne – also known as Holy Island – just off the coast of Northeast England. It was inhabited in the 7th century by Irish monks and became an important center of Christianity in the British islands until it was attacked and sacked by Viking raiders in 793.

Hmm. No more plowing through snowdrifts in the winter. Mae would be pleased, and I'm at the stage in life where blizzards hold less romanticism than they once did. And warm winters in Texas sounded good to me.

"What do you mean by 'ecumenical'? What is worship like?" I said, wincing and picturing rock bands and people with their hands waving in the air, definitely not my worship style or preference.

"Bishop Farley tells me it's actually very traditional. The island inhabitants are of an age where the latest and greatest trends don't impress them."

I didn't fall off the turnip truck yesterday, so I asked, "Are these parishes financially stable?" No way did I want to move halfway across the continent only to be without a position in a year.

"Let's just say the endowment funds feeding both will keep you and Mae, as well as the needs of the parishes, quite comfortable well into the 22nd century. Your good wife would not have to take a job to make ends meet."

"I've never heard of a hundred-year endowment. Where did the money come from?"

"Early investments in Minnesota iron ore and Texas oil."

I could feel my interest rising like incense at the Easter Vigil. "May I step out for a minute and call Mae?"

"No need. You stay here while I visit the sanctuary. My legs need stretching anyway."

Bishop McNally unwound his tall, thin frame and carried his coffee to St. Andrew's sanctuary while I called Mae's cell and explained the situation. She knew I was unhappy here and said her passport was ready and waiting. Cool summers and warm winters sounded good to her in the final decade of my ministry. She also stood ready to hang up her shingle as a high school history teacher. I could tell by her tone of voice she would gladly leave behind teenagers who didn't care about Charlemagne, Bonnie Prince Charlie, or the difference between the 16th century reformer Martin Luther and the 20th century civil rights leader Martin Luther King.

I clicked off and found the bishop sitting in the far back pew, his head bowed either in prayer or fatigue. His head rose when I slid into the pew next to him and said, "May we visit the place?"

"Certainly. I can arrange a meeting with the junior warden through Bishop Farley."

"How about the senior warden?"

"It seems the parish doesn't have one. They don't see the need, actually, so one person serves both roles. While many of the congregation's members are Episcopalian by birth or marriage, the parish seems to operate quite well with minimum oversight. Most of the members are, shall we say, not denominationally tied."

The older I got, the less I held interest in church politics or, for that matter, denominational allegiance. I'd had enough. A place that might simply consider itself "Christian," yet held to traditional worship, sounded perfect.

"Then please arrange a visit," I said. "We'll ready ourselves for the trip."

"Very well," said Bishop McNally. "I'll try to schedule the visit soon during week days, but if that's not possible I will find a priest to supply St. Andrew's for Sunday mass. Once you return, I'll need a decision within a week."

"That's not much time," I said.

"Knowing you and your situation here as I do, I think the decision is already made." He knew Mae and me well. Both sets of our parents had gone to their reward, and God had not blessed us with children, therefore no grandchildren to tie us to any certain locale.

"Thank you for understanding," I said. "You're an exemplary bishop."

"Thank you for that," said Bishop McNally, then added, "Oh, and one more thing. You're not allergic to cats, are you?"

Chapter 2

When Fearghus Dingle left Nova Scotia in 1877 and headed west in search of his fortune, he landed in an area that resembled his surname, "Dingle" meaning "wooded valley."

The central lakes region of north-central Minnesota, rich in wood, wildlife, and water, suited Fearghus, who had made somewhat of a name for himself in the east as a trapper of fur-bearing animals, but his inbred wanderlust found him in the idyllic surroundings of the North Star State.

He quickly set about building a small cabin on the shore of Bluestone Lake, trapping raccoon, mink, fox, and any other animal he could profit from, the women of the newly-settled area pining for fur coats and wraps. Employing local Ojibway youth for a pittance, in four years he was the wealthiest man in the area.

And yet the devout Episcopalian remembered his childhood in south-east Scotland, and how he romanticized the Holy Island of Lindesfarne and Saint Aidan, the Irish priest who built a cathedral on the island and converted the Anglo Saxons to Christianity in the 6th century A.D.

So Fearghus, at the age of 48, caused to be built, with the hesitant backing of the Episcopal diocese of Minnesota, the church of Saint Aidan's-on-the-Lake.

The "cathedral kirk," as Fearghus called it, built of native pine and covered in gray stones harvested from local farm fields and the shores of Bluestone Lake to make it look "officially Episcopal," became the principal landmark on the 30-acre island and, indeed, the expanding town of Bluestone.

Many in the area looked on this project as a Tower of Babel, referring to it as "Fearghus's Folly," but Fearghus would not be deterred, although he began to take a dram or two to help him forget their taunts. The dram or two eventually turned into a bottle or two, until *Fearghus* could most days be seen stumbling about, shouting incoherent instructions to the workmen constructing the church.

The kirk was no sooner built, paid for, and dedicated to the glory of God when an inebriated Fearghus Dingle died at the age of 52 in a duel with a local farmhand over which scotch was superior, Arran Robert Burns or Johnnie Walker Gold. He had spent everything he had on the church, and without further financial backing or even a congregation, the Episcopal diocese let the beautiful church of St. Aidan's-on-the-Lake wither and die in the early days of the 20*th* century, the legacy of a drunken trapper.

After the second World War, the country on the move, a far-sighted bishop saw the abandoned church and convinced the powers-that-be to resurrect St. Aidan's-on-the-Lake as an ecumenical summer parish/retreat similar to the Taizé community in France.

Substantial funds were raised from various sources – including investments in the taconite industry further north – creating an endowment fund in excess of a million dollars, quite the sum in the 1950s. Those funds were shrewdly invested by a Minneapolis firm and over time grew more than tenfold.

Herb Hampshire, a cradle Episcopalian and owner of the local lumberyard, heard of the plan and saw an opportunity. He offered to build rental cabins on the island, including all necessary infrastructure such as water, sewer, and electric. After recouping his investment and using the construction for a tax write-off as a charitable donation, he deeded the cabins to the Episcopal diocese of Minnesota.

He'd designed the island community like a wheel, the outer edge a walking trail with spoke-like pathways leading to each cabin. Shared boat docks protruded into the lake between every other cottage. Norway Pines, the state tree, circled the island behind the cabins separating them from the forested area between the church and the desired cabins that faced away from the town of Bluestone.

From 1990 to 2000 the island community was struggling. Cabin rentals were down, and the church had trouble obtaining a priest, until a call from the local bishop changed everything.

A parish in Texas full of retired snowbirds was looking for a suitable place to keep the community together during the hot southern summer months. The vestry of a parish in the Texas Hill Country visited St. Aidan's and was duly impressed, and so the dual parish of St. David's and St. Aidan's-on-the-Lake was formed.

The ruling committees, or vestries, of both congregations now began the process of looking for either two part-time priests or one full-time priest who would agree to serve both churches. The joint vestries contacted Episcopal bishops from all dioceses in North America and Canada.

Chapter 3

Our Tuesday flight to Minneapolis the second week in March was stimulating, if you consider screaming infants and chatty seatmates inspirational. I'd previously rented a car for the hour drive to Bluestone, so upon retrieving our carry-on bags from the overhead compartments and finding our way off the plane and into the concourse, we strode to the Avis booth and were given keys to a late model mid-size Ford.

The GPS app on my cellphone directed us to head north and west of the Twin Cities. Once we got off the interstate, we were struck by the simple beauty of the landscape. Deciduous trees mixed with evergreens lined the two-lane road.

As we drove, I recited the first stanza of the poem Bishop McNally referenced:

> *I will arise and go now, and go to Innisfree,*
> *And a small cabin build there, of clay and wattles made;*
> *Nine bean-rows will I have there, a hive for the honey-bee,*
> *And live alone in the bee-loud glade.*

"I certainly hope this island is not infested with bees," said Mae. "What could Yeats have been thinking? He was obviously not allergic to stings, as far as we know, Epipens not yet being invented," referring to the injectable drug used by people dreadfully allergic to bee stings.

"I'm sure all will be well," I said, hoping for the best, yet knowing that new environs always have their own set of challenges. My phone conversations with the junior warden had answered some of my initial questions.

"How will we get onto the island?" asked Mae. "Is there a causeway?"

"Apparently not. One of the locals runs a ferry from the mainland. Some island inhabitants have their own boats to shuttle back and forth for needed trips to town."

"What about cars?" said my suddenly inquisitive wife. While she was not lacking in faith, her practical side kept me on this side of reality.

"I'm told the local Ford dealership allows free parking a short walk from the town dock. No cars on the island."

The ever-faithful GPS app – who I'd named "Googleena" – directed us to the above-mentioned car dealership. After arriving at 11:00, I parked in the used car lot containing several cars with boat trailers attached and was immediately greeted by a sturdy man about six feet tall with short, brown hair, a two-day scruffy beard, and wire-rimmed glasses.

"You must be Pastor MacManus," said the man, offering a handshake.

"Actually, I prefer to be called Father MacManus. Once we get to know each other better you can call me what you like, as long as it's not late for dinner," I joked. "This is my wife, Mae."

"Dennis O'Neill at your service," said the man, bowing slightly to Mae. "Junior warden, actually the only warden, and all-around handy man at St. Aidan's."

We returned his greeting. "Is my rental car safe here?" I said. Mae looked up and down the street, checking out the environs.

"Absolutely. The crime rate in Bluestone is next to nil. Only the occasional group of rowdy teens feeling their oats. The car, and you, are perfectly safe. Now, please follow me and we'll stop for a quick lunch before visiting the island."

We walked and chatted for two short blocks. Dennis led is into a grocery store as Mae shot me a skeptical look I knew all too well.

"You must be wondering about lunch in a grocery store," said Dennis. "The Pick-Em-Up is the best stop in town," he said, leading us to a buffet counter stocked with sandwiches, salads, Chinese entrees, and more. "As you'll find out, the folks at St. Aidan's like to eat."

"This looks perfect," said Mae, always the diplomat, even though I knew she would have preferred a setting more sophisticated than plastic benches and faux-wooden tables.

"Hey, Ingrid! How's it goin'?" said Dennis to a girl behind the counter. Ingrid appeared to be in her early twenties, tall, blonde, and gorgeous in that Minnesota Scandinavian way. Even the cap/hairnet couldn't diminish her attractiveness.

"It's going good," said Ingrid. "What can I get for you, Mr. O'Neill?"

"This is Father MacManus and his wife Mae," said Dennis, motioning to us. "We're hoping he'll agree to be the new priest at St. Aidan's. Get them whatever they want and put it on my bill."

"Will do," said Ingrid. "Ladies first. What would you like?" she said, smiling at Mae.

"What's the local specialty?" said Mae.

"That would be lutefisk, but you're in luck. We don't serve it here, thanks be to God."

Mae had heard of lutefisk, and had been forewarned more than once not to eat it, ever.

"Then I'll have a turkey sub with lettuce and tomatoes," said Mae.

"Got it. And for you?" she asked me.

"The same, with a bowl of wild rice soup," I said.

"Excellent choice. Mr. O'Neill?"

"I'll have what the good father is having, only add some of those sweet peppers to my sandwich."

"Coming right up."

As Ingrid prepared our lunches, Mae wandered over to inspect the bouquets of carnations and miniature roses displayed near the checkout counter.

"We're very proud of Miss Ingrid Larssen," said Dennis, bringing a blush to the girl's cheeks. "She was the valedictorian of her high school class and just got her MBA from St. Olaf. Her dad owns this store along with several others in neighboring towns. He's prepping her for management, making her start at the bottom."

"Your father is a wise man," I said to Ingrid, bringing another smile and blush.

+ + +

After lunch, Dennis said, "Well, I imagine you're anxious to see the church and the island. Let me call Shorty." He pulled his cell from his pocket.

"Who is Shorty?" asked Mae.

"He's our cabby, but not in the traditional sense," said Dennis. "You'll see."

Dennis talked on his phone, then signed for our lunches and led us out to the street and three blocks east while he pointed out the various shops and points of interest on Bluestone's Main Street, including two banks, a barber shop, and a law office.

We arrived at a boat landing where a very tall, distinguished-looking man with elegant gray hair and Ray-Ban sunglasses stood smiling at Dennis. Behind him we could see St. Aidan's steeple in the middle of the forested island.

"Hey, Shorty. Thanks for being available. Would you take me and these two out to the island?"

"Sure. Follow me," he said, turning and walking to a pontoon boat tethered to a dock.

Shorty helped Mae on, then me, then Shorty got on as Dennis untied the pontoon and hopped aboard. Once we were settled on a bench at the back of the boat, Shorty revved the engine and set out. When Mae decided Shorty couldn't hear our conversation over the drone of the engine, she leaned over and said to Dennis, "Why is he called 'Shorty' when he's obviously not?"

Dennis chuckled and turned close to Mae. "His real name is Eugene Dvorak. When he was in elementary school, he was the runt of the class and got the nickname. After he sprouted in junior high and high school, it was too late to change it."

"He must have a good business in the summers running the ferry," I said.

"It's not a business," said Dennis. "After he retired as the town's postmaster two years ago, he got bored, so he does this for nothing. Says it keeps him sane."

+ + +

Shorty expertly pulled up at the main island dock, hopped off, and held the pontoon steady as we climbed off. Mae kept herself fit doing Pilates and Tai Chi, so she had no problem disembarking. I took a bit longer and was helped by a sturdy tug of the arm by Dennis.

"Thanks for the ride," I said to Shorty, who reached in his pocket, pulled out a plain white business card and handed it to me. I looked at the brief script:

Shorty
555-0173

"Any time," said Shorty. "You have my number."

Chapter 4

Dennis carried our overnight bags we'd retrieved from our rental car after lunch and led us about 10 meters down a paved, well-kept trail where he set our bags down and opened the front door to a little cottage, the church looming behind.

Dennis entered first and turned on the overhead light. When he carried our bags to what I assumed was the bedroom, we stood taking in the quintessential Northwoods lake home.

Mae, overwhelmed, said "This is just lovely! Look at that knotty pine paneling, and that fireplace, and the green trim, and the kitchen! Have I died and gone to heaven?" The new stainless-steel refrigerator and propane range/oven overwhelmed her. She undoubtedly remembered the rusty avocado 1970s appliances in the parsonage at St. Andrew's.

"You may not have much use for the kitchen," said Dennis, back from the bedroom. "As I said, we like to eat here on the island, which brings me to invite you to your first St. Aidan's shindig. Every Monday and Wednesday we serve breakfast and every Friday the church hosts a fish fry, the main course caught right here on Bluestone Lake. If you have the fishing bug, you're welcome to add to the catch, Father. You too, Mrs. MacManus. We don't discriminate. Some even say a lady's bait is more attractive to the fish."

"You've got that right," I said, winking and forming a fish mouth at Mae who tipped her head and rolled her eyes.

"I haven't fished since I was a boy, except for that one unfortunate ocean outing. Sea sickness is not something I'd like to revisit," I said.

"On Bluestone Lake you don't even have to get in a boat. Just buy an annual license, stand on the dock at your cabin of an evening and drop a line. The fish come to you."

"Really?"

"That's all there is to it, although some prefer to get in their boats and go to deeper water for the state fish."

"What's a state fish?" asked Mae.

"The walleye is actually *the* state fish. Plentiful in north country lakes. Walleye cheeks are a delicacy."

"Fish have cheeks?" she said, as I ambled around the one visible room, living, dining, and kitchen all-in-one.

"Yes, they do. Just don't get caught swiping too many on Friday. You might get your knuckles rapped," Dennis said with a smile.

"All this talk of fish reminds me of a poem by John Bunyan I learned as a lad," I said.

> *The water is the fish's element:*
> *Leave her but there, and she is well content.*
> *So's he, who in the path of life doth plod,*
> *Take all, says he, let me but have my God.*

"A wonderful poem for a priest," said Dennis.

"Not just for a priest, for all," I said.

"Now, Angus, I certainly hope you will not burden these good people with your love of obscure poetry," scolded Mae.

"They better get used to it," I said.

"I'll let you get settled," said Dennis. "I'll be back about 5:00. The vestry has a meal planned for you in the church fellowship hall. You'll have a chance to meet us and see a bit of the building."

"Is your cabin nearby?" I said.

"I don't live on the island. I'm a townie, along with my wife. She's Lutheran and has roots in Bluestone, so we maintain a home in town," he said. "See you about 5:00." He turned and left us to marvel at the lovely coziness of what could become our summer home should I accept this position.

14

As Mae inspected the kitchen appliances, I improvised a take-off on Yeats's poem:

I will arise and go now, and go to Bluestone Lake,
And have there a little cabin for my bonnie maid,
Surround ourselves with loch and the green pine tree
And live together in the Northland's shade.

"You are fortunate you've never been arrested for plagiarism," said Mae.

"I only paraphrase what's in the public domain," I said, hands in my pockets, rocking on my heels, admiring the northern Minnesota feel of the cottage.

Mae walked to the broad bay window overlooking the lake, and beyond, the town of Bluestone. She motioned to the stainless-steel side-by-side refrigerator and range/oven. "This is lovely," she said. "So far, I approve."

"So far?" I said. "Are you pessimistic?"

"No, not pessimistic. Realistic."

A wood-burning fireplace faced with fieldstones stood to the left of the entry door; a small loveseat angled toward the fireplace; a big-screen TV hung on the wall opposite the love seat. A small dining table for four divided the living space from the kitchen

We paused in our admiration of the cabin to stow our two-day wardrobes in the master bedroom's closet and dresser. A charming green duvet covered the Queen-sized bed; matching pillow shams snuggled against the bookcase headboard built from what looked like native wood. The bedroom walls, like the rest of the cabin, were paneled in knotty pine, keeping with the Northwoods feel of the place. The beige carpet looked and felt underfoot to be less than a year old.

The bath next to the bedroom appeared to have been recently updated. It contained a bright white commode, sink, and walk-in shower with an adjustable rain shower head. The walls were papered in green depicting a pine forest.

On the other side of the bathroom another smaller bedroom filled out the main floor. A bit smaller than the master, its appointments were equally as comforting. It also contained a stacked front-load washer and dryer.

"I could do with a nap. How about you?" I said.

"Ditto," said Mae. "Set the timer on your cell. It wouldn't do to sleep past dinner."

We flopped on the bed, I set my phone alarm, but didn't doze even one wink.

Chapter 5

True to his word, Dennis knocked on our door at 4:55. We were to learn that promptness, not always honored by some out east, is a Midwestern virtue.

He led us to a path that led to the church' side door. Down a short hallway we could smell deliciousness coming from the kitchen.

"This way, please," said Dennis, who led us into a large room filled with round, lightweight plastic tables, each surrounded by six chairs. I was impressed to see the chairs were not the standard metal folding type ubiquitous to most church halls. My backside said a silent prayer of thanks.

Three people – two women and one man – were seated at one of the tables. They all stood when Dennis led us to them.

"Ladies and gent, I'm pleased to introduce to you Father Angus MacManus and his wife, Mae. Father MacManus is checking us out to see if he's interested in serving St. Aidan's, so make a good impression! Please introduce yourselves."

I smiled and approached the first woman, skinny, sour faced, with wild hair, wearing winged cat-eye glasses, the kind that make you think you're always being inspected by a dour schoolmarm. She wore a threadbare blue flannel shirt, pedal pushers, and brown Red Wing boots.

"I'm Millie TerHorst," she growled in a voice that made me think she must have smoked for years. "I only agreed to be on the vestry so you Episcopalians don't go off the deep end with your hoity-toity ways."

"Nice to meet you, Millie. I can assure you my ways have never been known to be hoity or toity." She glowered at me and sat, crossing her stick-like arms in a defensive posture.

Dennis stood next to the other woman and said, "And this is Thelma Wadewitz, our organist." His voice rose about 40 decibels and said, "Thelma, this is Father MacManus."

Thelma stood about five feet tall, had gray curly hair, and a ready smile. She wore black flats, gray slacks, and a white blouse. She shook my hand and said, "Nice to meet you, but I never cared for star anise. It's poisonous in large doses, you know." Then she sat next to Millie who bent to her and blared in her ear. "You forgot your hearing aids!"

Thelma just smiled and said, "I know I'm a God-fearing old maid. You don't have to remind me, for heaven's sake."

Lastly a sturdy, tanned, man well over six-feet tall with a shock of white hair reached and shook my hand.

"John Smyth, with a 'y'," he said. He wore athletic shoes with no socks, tan cargo shorts, and a short-sleeved jean shirt, the weather somewhat unseasonably warm. Frameless reading glasses sat on the end of his nose.

"John is a good man to know," said Dennis. "He's a retired physician, but he still serves as the county coroner."

"That's true," said John. "Thankfully, a coroner's duty is very rarely needed in a county like Bluestone. These days I spend time with my wife and catch the occasional panfish off my deck."

"Nice to meet you, John," I said.

Suddenly a clamorous noise interrupted our conversation. I turned to see a man in a white chef's hat, matching white double-breasted jacket, and apron, pulling on a rope attached to a bronze bell mounted on the wall.

"And this is our esteemed chef, Malcolm Macalester, who with his wife Fiona have prepared our feast. Before we partake, would you lead us in a prayer, Father?" said Dennis.

"Certainly," I cleared my throat and said, "As you might surmise from my surname, I am of Scottish ancestry. Dennis has already tasted my love of poetry, so please allow me to offer this prayer written by Scotland's Robert Burns." All stood, folded their hands, and bowed their heads as I spoke in my preacher voice:

> *Some hae meat and canna eat,*
> *And some wad eat that want it,*
> *But we hae meat and we can eat,*
> *And so the Lord be thankit.*

John Smyth added a hearty "Amen." I turned to Malcolm and looked for instruction. He said, "Everyone be seated. It is our pleasure to serve you this evening." We sat as Malcolm and Fiona served us a most delicious meal of braised chicken breast, miniature potatoes, and Green Beans Almondine with Hollandaise sauce. Dessert consisted of Baked Alaska and some of the best coffee I'd ever tasted. Bishop McNally knew what he was talking about when he said this parish had no financial constraints.

After our plates had been cleared and we finished enjoying the coffee, Mae said, "This is my cue to leave you to business." She graciously stood to escape to the cabin and said, "It was nice meeting you all." The vestry, save Millie TerHorst, all responded in kind and waved her off.

Once she left, I said, "Is there anything you'd like to ask me, anything in particular you're looking for in a clergyman?" I recalled Bishop McNally mentioning the ecumenical nature of the parish.

Millie scowled and said, "I certainly hope you're not one of those 'smells and bells' papists."

"Bells only on a rare occasion," I said. "No smells. Incense gives me a headache." That seemed to satisfy her for now.

John Smyth said, "We tolerate pretty much anything, as long as the sermon doesn't last forever and a day."

"Fifteen minutes tops," I said. "Usually well under." He nodded slightly and smiled, then leaned over and spoke in Thelma's ear in his deep baritone. "Thelma, do you have a question for Father MacManus?"

"Oh, yes," she said, smiling like she'd just won the lottery. "Do you like Bach?"

"Very much," I said, as loudly as I thought necessary.

"Heaven help us," groaned Millie.

"Dennis, do you have any questions for me?" I said.

"Can you operate a wrench?" he said. I wasn't sure if he was joking or not.

"My mechanical aptitude peaked at screwdrivers," I said.

"That's OK," he said. "I can teach you."

After a few more inconsequential questions and comments, Dennis said, "Tomorrow Father MacManus will be shown the rest of the building and head back east on Thursday to determine his future. I think I speak for us all in saying we hope he will be with us in short order." The rest of the vestry stood and smiled, except Millie, who stood and frowned. John bid us a good evening and strode out of the hall like a man half his age, which I put at around 72. Thelma, apparently ecstatic at my love of Bach, virtually floated out the door. Millie grumped away.

"Well, I hope you thought that went well," said Dennis. "I hope you didn't take Millie too seriously. She's that way with everyone, not just you."

"Not at all," I said, thinking Millie obviously has some unspoken pain. "I'd love to get to know her better."

"She's been here ten summers and none of us can melt her."

"Should I be led to be her spiritual advisor at St. Aidan's, I will do as the Scripture says and as I imagine you have all been doing: bear one another's burdens and so fulfill the law of Christ."

"Amen to that," he said. "I trust you'll have a restful evening. I'll be back tomorrow morning for breakfast at 7:00 and then to show you the rest of the physical plant.

"I look forward to it." Dennis bid me farewell and left.

On my way out, I stopped in the kitchen to thank the chefs. Malcolm and Fiona both looked a bit young to be retirees, but then again it seems this parish could afford to hire them and provide housing.

"Thank you so much for dinner," I said. "It was all delicious."

Malcolm smiled and said, "Thank you, Father. It is our duty and delight to serve you."

"I understand you'll be serving breakfast tomorrow morning. I trust you have something equally delectable planned."

Fiona gazed at me, an enigmatic smile on her lips, dark hair trailing under her white chef's hat.

"You'll have to come and see," said Malcolm, looking like the cat who swallowed the canary.

Chapter 6

Nearly every chair in St. Aidan's Fellowship Hall was taken when Mae and I stepped in at 7:15 Wednesday morning. Before we could gather ourselves, Malcolm met us at the kitchen door and motioned us in. "You should be honored, Father," he said.

"Why is that?" I asked. Mae looked over my shoulder at Fiona, busy at the stove top.

Then I sniffed the air and said, "Can it be? Is that ... ?" Fiona stepped behind Malcolm, her chin up, eyes blazing.

"Bloody government here won't allow sheep's lungs," she practically shouted, "but we have our ways around that."

"Normally we only serve it on Half Burns night," said Malcolm. "Since we're not here on January 25, the day of Rabbie's birth, we celebrate the half-day in July, but today we've broken with tradition in your honor."

I was no great fan of Scotland's national dish, but I thanked them heartily anyway. Haggis, to many expatriate Scots, is like lutefisk to Norwegians – better honored than ingested. Today I would swallow my disgust and as much haggis as I could manage.

A red-haired woman flitted from table to table, talking and carrying dirty dishes to the open kitchen window as Mae and I carried plates past warming trays filled with real cheesy scrambled eggs, bacon, toast, and haggis. We had just picked up cups of coffee when the red-haired woman glided to us and said, "Are you our new priest you're our new priest aren't you I'm Penny Burns anything you want you just let me know how are you enjoying Bluestone I just love, love, love it here ... "

I waited for a break in the narrative and finally said, "Nice to meet you, Penny. This is my wife, Mae."

With that Penny was off again with a torrent of words that left us speechless. Eventually we broke away, found two empty chairs and introduced ourselves to a pleasant looking woman with blonde hair tied back in a French braid. She stood and said, "I'm Bonnie Paulson, from town. I never miss the food on the island." She motioned for us to sit, so we did.

Bonnie continued: "Malcolm and Fiona are wizards. They could work for any four-star restaurant in the state." After the meal Monday night and the food this morning, (even the haggis) I had to concur.

After we finished breakfast, Mae stayed and chatted with Bonnie while Dennis confiscated me for a short tour of the building. He was obviously proud of his hand in caring for it. The sanctuary, breathtaking like the outside of the building, was well-kept, with dark, oiled pews, red carpet, and a stained-glass window portraying Christ's nativity above the altar. Other windows surrounding the nave depicted various saints, including St. Aidan.

"We have a cleaning lady come in from town once a week. She does a good job," said Dennis, strolling down the main aisle, "and Penny Burns makes sure of it by cleaning up after the cleaning lady."

"Really? Penny must be OCD," I said, recalling our introduction to the talkative woman.

"I think obsessively compulsive is just the tip. Come, we didn't have time to see the office yesterday. Follow me."

We walked out the back of the nave, past a reception desk, and through a door with a sign on it saying RECTOR. Dazzled does not begin to show my impression of the office that would be mine should I accept this position. Compared to the converted janitor closet in Bicker Harbour, this was paradise: walls paneled in light oak, spongey carpet, a mahogany desk the size of North Dakota; a flat-screen TV mounted on the wall across from the desk on which rested an Apple MacBook Pro, apparently new since the box it came in rested next to it. A wireless printer sat on the ledge behind the desk.

"We thought a new priest deserved a new computer. Father Watson was far from technologically literate, satisfied with pen, paper, and his antique manual typewriter." Dennis beamed, proud of the vestry's plans to attract me.

"I'm dumbstruck," I said, and said no more, staring at the state-of-the-art furnishings.

"A good sign," said Dennis. "Not often is clergy at a loss for words. The whole building has undergone significant upgrades over the years, thanks to the endowment."

"How much is the fund worth now?" I said, feeling if I were to serve here, I'd have a right to know."

Dennis said, "St. Aidan's fund is more than a half billion and less than a billion, as of last accounting. I'm told the parish in Texas is similarly well-endowed."

"Did you say 'billion' with a 'b'?"

"Yessir," said Dennis.

"I ... I simply don't know what to say."

"Good. Let me show you the secretary's office." He led me to a room next to the rector's office. File cabinets lined the wall across from a desk. The rest of the room looked like any professional office at any highly rated institution.

Dennis said, "We've always thought it best to hire someone not a member of the congregation to take care of the business side of things. Maureen does a great job and only needs to come in on Wednesdays to write any necessary checks and look after our investments, and Friday mornings to prepare the service folders for Sunday mass, at your direction, of course. She only attends vestry meetings when necessary, which is to say seldom."

"Sounds like things run like a well-oiled machine," I said.

"We like to think so. Of course, when you leave in the fall for Texas, that parish has its own setup. The residents here who spend winters there seem to like it. When you return in the spring, this will be waiting as you see it."

"How many island residents go south in the fall?" I asked.

"Some, including a few from town," said Dennis. "Some hearty souls stay behind in Minnesota or neighboring states, but not many. The draw of warm weather seems to be magnetic. It's really an ideal situation, especially for our aging population like me. Those few who stay behind say winter here keeps the riff-raff out."

"But you have a house in town," I said, "so you stay, right?"

"No, Trudy and I decided to be snowbirds several years ago. We lock up the house, give the keys to our kids here and hop in our motor home to our daughter in California come October."

+ + +

That evening Dennis took us by his boat to the mainland where he and his wife, Trudy, treated us to a delectable dinner at Lyla's, an upscale restaurant.

"I'm afraid you won't see me too often at St. Aidan's," said Trudy, another tall, blonde Scandinavian. "I serve on the altar guild and sing in the choir at Trinity Lutheran in town."

"I love Lutherans!" I said. "They remind the rest of us Christians to check our beliefs with the Holy Scriptures."

"Sometimes even Lutherans need to be reminded of that," said Trudy, laughing and smiling. "Mae, if you're interested, a group of women from Bluestone meet once a month at Trinity to sew quilts and baby blankets. Coffee and sweets are treated almost as equal with Holy Communion."

Mae put on her biggest smile and said, "I'd be thrilled and honored to be a part of your group, should Angus accept the position at St. Aidan's."

That all but sealed the deal for me.

Chapter 7

"This is absolutely lovely," I said as Mae and I walked the trail around the island later that Wednesday evening. In mid-March, dirty snow still bordered the path, but while the evening air still had a bit of a chill, the slushy remains would not be long for this world.

"'Tis better than most," she said, thinking of other places we'd been. "Just look at the pines. Do you smell that?"

We stopped to soak in the beauty of the breezeless evening. Tomorrow our flight back to Bicker Harbour departed at 2:00 p.m., arriving in Nova Scotia by 7:00. I'd already booked Shorty Dvorak's water taxi for a ride to town at 9:00 a.m.

I hated to think of leaving this place.

"It smells a bit like Christmas," I said, smiling and reaching for her hand. Mae turned to look at me. She always called my gap-toothed grin "endearing." I found it repulsive. My frugal parents, God rest their souls, did not believe in or have the wherewithal, for that matter, to send me to an orthodontist. Over time, I perfected a closed-mouth smile around everyone but Mae. She was probably lying about admiring my choppers. I let her.

Mae was born in Boston, I in Toronto. We met at McGill University in Montreal where I studied theology, earning my bachelor and Master of Divinity degrees, while Mae studied education, planning to teach secondary history. We married after I finished my studies and I embarked on a career as an Episcopal clergyman. We both held dual citizenship, making the move to Bluestone and St. David's in Texas simple. So far, they looked like the perfect places to serve before retirement. Since St. Aidan's and St. David's were a dual parish, as it were, I saw no need to visit Texas.

Mae pestered me gently and regularly regarding my lack of exercise. Over the years my sporadic regimen had devolved into walking when I had the time, which was seldom. No calisthenics, weights, stretching, Pilates, or yoga for me. I was satisfied with my relative inactivity and my comfortable roundness. Mae, though, believed it all, keeping a rigorous schedule of physical activity, maintaining her girlish figure, all the better for me.

"And look at that water. Much calmer than the Atlantic," I said, nodding to the calm lake visible through the pines.

"And much warmer than the Atlantic coast," said Mae, enjoying the mid-60s temperature on this pleasant evening.

"Aye, 'tis warmer," I said, squeezing her hand and leading her finally to our cabin's lake dock. Before the sun set, we stood above the water, Bluestone Lake a mirror, not a breeze stirring. And strangely, not a bird chirping.

The linnets, or sparrows as they were called here, were normally merrily singing their evensong at this time, but oddly, not a sound could be heard until a chill gust riffled across the surface of the lake, and just like that, the temperature dropped fifteen degrees.

"We better take cover against this ill wind," I said, turning and gently pushing Mae off the dock and then up the incline to our cabin. Black clouds hovered northwest of the lake. We entered our cottage and turned on the lights as Mae pulled a multi-colored Indian blanket off the back of a vintage wooden rocking chair and threw it over her shoulders against the sudden chill, her dark hair falling across the wool.

"Check the radio or telly for weather warnings," I said as the power went off, rendering the radio and TV useless. In the waning daylight, I began a fire in the fireplace, making sure to open the flue lest we fill the cabin with smoke. Suddenly darkness enveloped the island, then pea-sized hail descended, transforming our lovely evening stroll into a reminder of how life can change in an instant.

+ + +

The sudden storm notwithstanding, after our return trip on Thursday I gave my notice at St. Andrew's and closed up shop at the parsonage. We sold outright or donated most of our belongings, the cabin at Bluestone furnished to our liking, moving with money in our pockets better than shipping loads of possessions halfway across the continent. If we did want new things, we could buy them and have the distinguished Shorty Dvorak transport them across the tide.

And so, my gentle slide into retirement began.

Chapter 8

Once I was duly installed at St. Aidan's by Bishop Farley the first Sunday in April, Mae and I entered into the hard but satisfying work of getting settled in the rector's cabin. We kept Shorty Dvorak busy shuttling us back and forth into town for necessary supplies.

After Malcolm and Fiona's delicious breakfast the first Monday after my installation, I set out at 9:00 in the morning, learning the lay of the land. I kept on my black clergy shirt and "dog collar" under a gray blazer, lest the residents think I was a prowling criminal. I walked the pleasant trail circling the island, a trek that would have taken less than an hour if not for frequent stops to introduce myself to those who ventured out of their cabins that cool spring morning, like Penny Burns who stepped out of a green cabin, scurrying to greet me.

"Good morning, Father!" she gushed, taking and squeezing my hand, her eyes and smile wide. She bobbed up and down like a silly school girl.

She released my hand, stepped back, and said, "I'm Penelope Burns we've met but really didn't have much time to get acquainted everyone calls me Penny, although I'm not cheap if you know what I mean. What am I saying, talking improperly to clergy! What I mean is I'm just Penny. Happy, happy Penny Burns I love everyone and I hope they all love me ..." She went on for another what seemed to me like an hour.

Attempting to change the narrative, I finally interjected saying, "Pardon me for saying, but you don't look old enough to be of retirement age. I was told the residents of the island were pensioners."

"Oh, I'm not that old but Harry retired last year when he turned 60 he worked very hard and has a good annuity from his company he was very well-paid so I never had to work. His name is Harrison but everybody calls him Harry just like I'm Penelope but everybody calls me Penny isn't that a hoot? Harry worked for an internet company so he could work from his computer anywhere in the world wherever he wanted and that's how we ended up here on Bluestone just this March we've been all kinds of interesting places you'll be at the fish fry this Friday, won't you?" She stared at me with an expectant, puppy dog look, panting after her continuous discourse.

"Wouldn't miss it," I said, trying to break eye contact.

"I'll see you then," she purred, lifting her long hair behind her right ear. "It starts at 5:00 and ends at 8:00. Don't be late! Hey, that's a poem!"

"Yes, yes, it is. Well, see you then," I said, smiling and taking a step back and turning to be on my way, breaking the force field that was Penny Burns.

+ + +

I was impressed with how well-kept all the cabins, lawns, and small flower gardens on the island were. Almost all the yards were decorated with moss roses, marigolds, or other colorful foliage. Some homes had window boxes overflowing with bright red geraniums.

Fiona Macalester stepped out of her cabin's front door, letting the screen door slap behind her. She had dark hair streaked with whisps of grey tied back with a red ribbon and was dressed in a red tartan jacket over a white shirt and black slacks. She was followed by Malcolm, dressed in dark brown khakis and a white button-down shirt.

"Hullo, Father," said Malcolm. "We met a few weeks ago at your visit. Just to review, I'm Malcolm, and this is my wife, Fiona, clan Macalester."

"Ah, yes! I remember. Fellow Scots, I see."

"Aye," said Malcolm, "and proud of it."

"I understand. I cherish my heritage as well, although three generations removed from the land of the brave." Fiona stood frowning behind Malcolm.

"My wife is not always the typical talkative Scotswoman," said Malcolm, "but you'll be hearing from her plenty on Wednesday eves."

"How is that, Fiona?" I said, tilting my head to smile at her, even showing my gap, trying to elicit a response.

"Let's let Wednesday evenings be a surprise, Father. You'll also see plenty of us in the kitchen at St. Aidan's, of course," said Fiona. "Malcolm's the cooker and I'm the baker."

"Half Burns night is coming soon enough," said Malcolm. "Haggis, neeps and tatties. Neeps and tatties are mashed potatoes and root vegetables, if you didn't know."

Robert Burns, three centuries dead, is still considered Scotland's national poet. Even the least cultured remember him, even if they don't know it, every New Year's Eve on hearing the familiar strains of "Auld Lang Syne" sung to the traditional old Scottish folk song.

"Very well, Malcolm. I'll look forward to it, and Fiona, allow me to say I'm fond of blueberry pie." Her face softened slightly before she said, "I will do my best, even though you are Anglican.

"Fiona was brought up the old way, and still holds to it," said Malcolm. "If it were up to her, everyone on the island would be Presbyterian."

+ + +

The freshly cut lawn at the next cabin couldn't negate the feeling I had standing in front of it. No flowers lined the walk. The window boxes were empty. Every exterior inch was painted gray without another color for variety. The whole place simply felt dour. As soon as I knocked on the screen door, I realized why.

Millie TerHorst, somewhere on the far side of 70 by my estimation, opened the inside door, glowered at me and said, "What do you want?"

"Actually, I'd like to make your further acquaintance," I said, giving her my best gap-toothed smile. "We didn't get much chance to talk when I was here earlier meeting with the vestry."

She was not about to invite me in, so I peeked over her shoulder at the cabin's living room decorated in a couch from the 1970s upholstered with People magazines, a coffee table adorned with a dozen or so Styrofoam cups and an overflowing ash tray.

"I'll have you know I'm a cradle Presbyterian," she said, "not one of those hoity-toity, chardonnay-sucking Episcopal broads."

"Good to know," I said.

"You'll see plenty of me because I'll be watching you." With that, she shut the door in my face.

+ + +

The next cabin was as opposite of the previous as a daisy from crabgrass. The flower boxes overflowed with colorful blooms, the door painted cherry red, the main façade sky blue. The welcome mat displayed the standard word bordered in yellow smiley faces.

Thelma Wadewitz wore dungarees, a blue long-sleeved denim shirt, Crocs slip-on sandals on bare feet, gardening gloves, and a large sun hat. She was on her knees weeding a small flower garden just off her stoop.

Not wanting to startle her, I cleared my throat and then said, "Hello," in a normal, non-preacher voice. When she didn't respond, I tried again in my preacher voice.

"HELLO THERE!"

She stopped weeding, put her hand trowel in a bucket, lifted her head, glanced at my clergy collar, smiled, hopped to her feet, and said, "Father MacManus! So nice to see you. I'm Thelma Wadewitz, the organist at St. Aidan's." She bubbled with enthusiasm, her unlined face putting her age at about 70 tops. Maybe she forgot we'd met earlier.

"Please come in," she said, slipping out of her gardening shoes and holding the door open for me. I stepped in to a delightfully-decorated space. A love seat like the one in our cabin, a wingback arm chair, and a cloth-upholstered glider rocker sat angled towards the fireplace. A kitchenette lay beyond a small foldout table with two wooden chairs, the layout basically the same as our cabin. Colorful paintings of flowers and outdoor scenes hung on every available wall space.

"I see that besides an organist you are also artistic," I said, motioning to the paintings as Thelma motioned me to sit in the arm chair while she moved to the glider rocker.

"Oh, I've never been arthritic. Just the occasional aches and pains that come with aging. At 92 that's to be expected."

"Certainly not!" I said. "You don't look a day over ..." She had the look of one or those ageless women who would be active past age 100.

Wait. Did I mention arthritis?

Thelma frowned and said, "I prefer the bus or train. Too many layovers at airports. At my age, wasted time is an abomination."

Hmm. I leaned towards Thelma and enunciated now in my loudest preacher voice, "Tell me about the organ."

"I've never owned a gun and never plan to. Have you been in the sanctuary to see the organ? It's a splendid Casavant, built just north of the border in Quebec. I just love playing it."

I shook my head, then slowly stood, approached Thelma and said, "It's been nice ..."

"Oh yes," she interrupted. "I never miss our Friday fish fries. I always practice organ after each one."

She stood, walked me to the door, smiled and said, "See you Friday. Save some tartar sauce for me."

I walked to the next cabin pondering the last two visits, thinking about the crabbiest person I'd ever met and a nonagenarian hard-of-hearing organist.

+ + +

Three cabins down from Thelma Wadewitz, a man the picture of Minnesota chic sat reading a newspaper on his front porch. He wore a dark blue polo shirt tucked into tan khakis, Dockers on his feet. He sat in an Adirondack chair, his legs crossed at the knee, smoke curling from a pipe dangling from the corner of his lips, his perfectly styled sandy haircut spoke of money and class, of a man who had retired well. A flabby Basset Hound lay contentedly next to him.

"Good morning!" I called from the bottom step leading up to his porch. He turned to see his visitor, uncrossed his legs, stood, put the paper and pipe on the chair, and walked down to meet me. He was fit in the way of men who live in exclusive suburbs. The Basset smiled at me but did not bother getting up.

"A beautiful day so far, isn't it?" he said, offering his hand and saying, "Tom Cooper."

I shook his hand and said, "Angus MacManus. Pleased to meet you."

He glanced at my collar, then at my eyes, and said, "You must be the new priest at St. Aidan's."

"Aye, that I am. Have you been living on the island long, Tom?"

He released my hand, glanced down, then back up and said, "Three summers. Won't you come in? Would you like something to drink?"

"Water would be fine. The humidity seems to be rising along with the temperature."

He led me to his cabin, opened the door, and we entered a space with the same floor plan as the others I'd seen. I imagine the builder simply picked one and repeated it.

"Why don't we sit at the table? Would you like ice?"

"Yes, please." My collar was starting to chafe. Rivulets of sweat ran down my spine and began soaking my black short-sleeved clergy shirt on this warming late spring morning.

I looked around the cabin while Tom got ice out of the refrigerator. I shouldn't generalize, but the decor showed a woman's touch. Several pictures hung on the wall of Tom with an astonishingly beautiful woman, the two obviously in love with each other. None of children, however.

Tom put two coasters and two glasses of ice water on the table, his movements graceful, almost athletic. He sat opposite me and looked in my eyes, a hint of a smile on his lips. We both took a sip and I said, "I noticed you have a boat at your dock. Are you a fisherman?"

"Not really, although I have been known to wet a line. It's there more as a convenience if I need to go into town. Faster than calling for a ride."

I nodded and said, "So, Tom, this cabin and those photos are charming. Is your wife about?"

Tom wrapped his hands around his water glass, stared at it for a moment, then looked back up at me and said, "I'd done quite well in my profession as an investment broker. When Jennifer retired from General Mills three years ago, I discovered Bluestone Lake. We were never blessed with children to spend our money on, so instead of renting, I bought her this place as a retirement gift. She'd always talked about wanting a lake home, but we never got around to getting one. Too busy."

"Yes," I said. "Life has a way of delaying our dreams."

"Yes, well, we only got to enjoy this together for one year. She died of ovarian cancer after our first summer here."

"I am so sorry," I said, shocked and sad at the same time.

"The disease progressed rapidly. She didn't suffer long."

Even though I'd just met Tom Cooper, my sense of empathy nearly overwhelmed me. I'd often wondered what I'd do if I'd lost Mae. Moisture grew under my eyelids joining the sweat on my spine.

"I am so, so sorry," I repeated. "Please let me know if you ever need to talk. I'm in the business of listening. I try to limit talking to Sunday mornings."

"Thank you, Father," said Tom. "I'll remember that. Worship at St. Aidan's has been a blessing to me when I feel up to attending. I'm glad you were able to fill the vacancy quickly," referring to my predecessor, Father Watson, who had finally fully retired after suffering a mild stroke.

We drank more water and simply sat in silence for a time.

"I wonder if you could answer a question for me regarding the island," I said.

"Certainly."

"You were reading a newspaper when we met. Did you go into town for it, or was it delivered?"

"Have you met Shorty Dvorak?" I nodded yes. "He delivers mail here, sort of a small-town arrangement, and probably not entirely legal. The postmaster puts all the island mail, including my subscription to the St. Paul Pioneer Press, in a bin. Shorty picks it up, brings it to the island."

"Is it brought to the church?" I asked, since the kirk serves as a community center as well as the house of worship.

"Actually, it's given to a resident who delivers it. Have you met Penny Burns?"

"I have indeed," remembering the talkative woman.

"Penny has to be the most helpful person in Bluestone, if not the whole state of Minnesota," said Tom. "If anything needs doing, she's the first to volunteer. She's quite the go-getter. She delivers the mail to all us islanders."

"A good person to know," I said. "Another question, if you don't mind."

"Shoot."

"Do you know the woman who lives in the gray cottage? Older lady, smokes cigarettes?"

"You didn't mention 'has an unpleasant personality.'"

"Yes, well ..."

"I'm sure Millie has a good side, but nobody has seen it as long as I've been here. We've all tried the pleasant approach, but she's not having it."

"Perhaps if we keep trying, she'll eventually sweeten."

"Don't hold your breath, Father."

Tom got up to answer a scratching at the door. He opened it and the aforementioned Basset Hound hopped in, bounded to me, put his forepaws on my lap, looked up at me, tongue lolling, ears hanging.

"Otis, down," said Tim. The dog immediately obeyed. "So sorry, Father. Otis is nothing if not friendly."

"No worries," I said, reaching down to let the hound smell my knuckles, which he then licked, so I gave him an ear scratch.

"He definitely has taken to you," said Tom. "He has always been able to distinguish friend from foe."

"I am honored to meet you, Otis," I said, looking down at the hound. "I hope we become fast friends." He panted and wagged, the polar opposite to Millie TerHorst.

"He has been a good pal to me, especially after Jennifer died," said Tom.

Tom was still obviously grieving.

"How do you spend your time?" I asked.

"I read, keep up on world events, walk Otis, and, oh yes, I'm the unofficial groundskeeper on the island of a sort."

I looked at him, puzzled.

"I cut lawns and do minor yard work for those who ask," he said.

"Good for you. Physical activity can have a beneficial effect on body and spirit. I hope I can rely on you to keep my yard trim," I said.

"Of course, Father."

Then I said, "I've heard much about the Friday fish fries. Do you attend?"

"Wouldn't miss it," he said, scooping dog food from a bin in the kitchen into a bowl. Otis ambled over and scarfed his food in less than 20 seconds, then sat at his master's feet.

"We'll see you Friday then," I said, standing to leave, shaking Tom's hand and scratching Otis's ear again.

The muse struck as I strolled from Tom's cabin to the next:

God said, "This is what I intend:
To give to man a best friend.
When he needs cheering up,
I will send him a pup.
He'll be all the more blessed in the end."

38

Not my best, but something, anyway.

+ + +

I noticed that each cabin on the island shared a T-shaped dock with its neighbor. Two swivel deck chairs were attached to the T of the next cabin's dock, the chairs occupied by an older couple dressed for the season in shorts and light shirts, sipping coffee and gazing at the lake.

I stood at the base of the dock, cleared my throat, and gave out a hullo.

They both swiveled their chairs toward me as John Smyth stood and said, "Permission granted to come aboard."

I should have recognized John, but seeing him from behind prevented me. I stepped onto the dock and made my way to the couple, who smiled in greeting.

"Good morning," I said, facing the two, hands at my side. I'm old fashioned enough to be reticent about offering a handshake to a woman in the company of another man. Since I'd already met John, I spoke to the woman I assumed was his wife. "I'm Angus MacManus, the new priest at St. Aidan's."

"Nice to meet you, Father. I'm Isabelle Smyth. Everyone calls me 'Belle.'" She stood with some difficulty, moved slowly to her husband, and took his arm.

"It's very nice to meet you, Belle. I'm making my way around the island today, introducing myself and getting to know the residents."

"Excellent," said John. "Belle, it's almost lunchtime. Father, won't you join us for a bite?"

"I wouldn't want to put you to any trouble," I said.

"No trouble at all," said Belle, smiling under a large sun hat similar to her husband's, still holding John's arm. "I hope you like chicken salad. Let's go inside. I'll get lunch ready while you two chat."

Arm in arm, the Smyth's led me slowly down the dock and up to their cabin. I couldn't help noticing how gently John helped Belle up the stairs and through the door, asking if she needed any help and if she'd be OK. Once she was safely in, John said, "Let's go back to the dock. No sense wasting a glorious day."

He turned and marched towards the chairs leaving me to follow as best I could. He nodded to his wife's chair for me to take a seat. He quickly sat next to me and said, "You undoubtedly noticed Belle has some trouble walking. The ravages of age and arthritis."

"Yes, well, if God grants us many years, we can't escape life's difficulties."

"True that," said John.

"Please tell me about your life in medicine," I said, recalling our introduction at my initial visit to Bluestone.

"I'd been in general practice for fifty years, so am well acquainted with 'life's difficulties' as you put it. I finally retired, but like many, was asked to stay on in a reduced capacity."

"Do you still see patients?"

"In a sense," he chuckled. "I agreed to stay on as coroner in a county that rarely has need of that service. In the last five years, I've only conducted two official inquests."

"Fascinating," I said.

"You wouldn't think that if you had to observe an actual autopsy. It's not for the squeamish."

"No, I'll stick to ministering to the living, thank you."

"From time to time I'm asked to look at simple problems on the island. I can't prescribe medication, but I can point people in the right direction and direct the occasional poor soul who gets into a patch of poison ivy to a bottle of calamine lotion."

"Do you miss practicing medicine?" I asked.

"I miss the patients. I don't miss the modern paperwork/computer screen jungle. Many a good physician has given up rather than spend inordinate amounts of time satisfying some bean counter," he said. "Well, enough complaining. Belle's chicken salad awaits."

With that, he stood and stepped lively to the cabin, leaving me in his wake.

+ + +

After stopping by to tell Mae I'd had lunch with the Smyths, I headed to my office, anxious to begin preparations for next Sunday's mass. I walked down the side aisle, hoping Thelma Wadewitz, who was butchering a heavy-handed prelude, wouldn't notice me from her perch on the organ bench in the east transept, just to the side of the lectern/reading stand. No such luck.

"Father! What a pleasant surprise! Do you like Elgar?" referring to the composer of the piece she'd been slaughtering.

"Very much," I shouted.

"Edward Elgar wasn't Dutch. He was English," she shouted back.

I waved and went on my way, leaving Thelma to her practice. I opened the door to the rector's office and was greeted by a large tabby cat perched on my desk. I froze as the cat stopped licking its paws and stared at me in that way cats have of displaying superiority over the human race. It won the staring contest, then lazily jumped off the desk and exited the study leaving through a hatch in the door leading to the memorial garden. I followed it out and caught Dennis working on the front door.

"Dennis, a cat seems to have made itself at home in my study."

"Was it a big tabby?" he asked.

"Yes."

"That's Cranmer. Pay him no mind. He's self-sufficient."

I remembered Bishop McNally asking me if I was allergic to cats. It seemed Cranmer had quite a reputation.

"Well, I'm not used to having a cat as an office mate."

"You'll get used to it. The congregation loves him."

"Who does he belong to?" I asked.

"It appears someone either didn't want the cat and dropped him off here to fend for himself about five years ago, or he jumped ship, wandered off, and his owners couldn't find him, so he was abandoned."

"What does he do in the winter?" I said.

Dennis smiled, turned his head, looked down and to the left and said, "He stays with my kids and grandkids."

"That's very kind of them to take in one of God's creatures," I said.

"They're not all that generous, Father. Cranmer gives as well as he gets. A cat in the house lying by the fire on long winter nights has its benefits."

"Yes, I suppose it does, if the beast is agreeable," I said.

"He is," said Dennis. "He's no trouble at all, and the grands love him."

Maybe I'll schedule "All Things Bright and Beautiful" by Cecil Alexander as the processional hymn some Sunday and have Cranmer present when we sing:

> All things bright and beautiful,
> All creatures great and small,
> All things wise and wonderful,
> The Lord God made them all.

Mrs. Alexander will probably be smiling down from heaven at her poetry, but I will reserve judgement on the cat.

Chapter 9

I'd asked for contact information from everyone I'd met so far, sharing cell numbers, save from Thelma Wadewitz who was too old-fashioned and stuck in the '60s, and Millie TerHorst, who told me in no uncertain terms she did not and would not ever own one of those brain-tumor inducing devices, and if she did, she certainly wouldn't give out her number, nor did she own one of those "I've fallen and I can't get up" gizmos.

After working on my sermon for two hours, I was about written and visited out, so I headed back to our cabin. Mae was busy arranging the kitchen drawers and cupboards. I filled her in on my day and she filled me in on hers.

"If you don't mind, before dinner I'd like to take my own walkabout and find a quiet spot in the woods for my exercises." Mae was into Tai Chi, which I didn't understand in the least, but it made her happy and kept her hale.

"You might want to bring some insect repellant along. The first generation of this year's mosquitoes are bound to be hatching soon."

"I'm way ahead of you," she said, taking a small bottle out of the cupboard. "Smell." She opened the bottle and held it to my nose.

"It smells like an ice cream cone," I said. "And that will repel biting insects?"

"Vanilla extract works just as well as those chemical sprays containing DEET. I read it on Facebook."

"Well, if you read it on Facebook … "

"I'm giving it a shot. I'd rather smell like this than a toxic waste dump," she said, dabbing some on her face, neck, and arms. Then she gave me a peck on the cheek and ventured into the midday sun.

Since I was free from spousal responsibility for the time being, I took off my spectacles, splashed cold water on my face, dried it with the forest green towel Mae had hung in the bathroom – a misnomer since the small room did not contain a bathtub, just a sink, commode, and shower.

I grabbed my briefcase and put a cardboard box under my arm, stepped out of the door, shut it behind me, circled behind the cabin on the well-kept lawn, and set out on the pathway to the kirk, where I met Dennis O'Neill still adjusting the front door. Organ music sounded in the sanctuary.

"Good day, Dennis. Looks like you're hard at it," I said.

He put down his screwdriver on the top of his stepladder, descended, and said, "Always something needing fixing, adjusting, or replacing in a building."

"Well, you seem to be the right man for the job. Where did you learn the necessary skills?"

"Thirty-five years as superintendent of maintenance at Bluestone schools. Before that, my father made sure I knew my way around a toolbox."

I put my briefcase and the box of books down and said, "May I have your cell number?" reaching in my pocket for my phone, not remembering if I'd entered it into my contacts earlier.

"It's on your desk. Call whenever you need me. And you'll see Trudy and me almost every Friday night for the fish fry." He licked his lips and gave a thumbs up.

"Yes, the Macalesters are top-notch cooks."

I picked up my briefcase and the box of books, Dennis held the door for me, and I entered the sanctuary to an overly-loud, fractured rendition of the alternate national anthem of Great Britain, "Land of Hope and Glory."

Chapter 10

On the long drive from Nova Scotia to Minnesota, we stopped in Rhinelander, Wisconsin for gas and a few supplies. I was amazed to see that the C-store carried beer, more specifically Cinnaster Scotch Ale, brewed in Green Bay.

"Well, this is serendipitous," I thought, putting two six packs of the brew on the checkout counter next to Mae's bag of chocolate covered peanuts, one of her guilty pleasures. The beer would go directly into the refrigerator once we'd reached Bluestone in a few hours.

I'd found that a little ale helped me concentrate while writing homilies. Maybe there was something to the research behind alcohol and journalistic excellence. I was not alcoholic, not by any means, but a few sips connected to the old country did put me in the mood for writing, especially poetry. Sometimes I fancied myself a link in the long chain of renowned Scottish writers:

Walter Scott ... Robert Burns ...
Hugh MacDairmid ... Angus MacManus ...

"Enough daydreaming," I said to myself. "On with the business at hand." I opened the box I'd carried from our cabin and took out the usual desk paraphernalia: scissors, pencils, paper clips, Post-it notes, and the pen Mae gave me at my first assignment. She'd had the costly Montblanc monogrammed with my initials – "A I M" for Angus Ian MacManus – mounted on a marble base. It always rested on my previous desks, and now this one, in a place of honor within easy reach. I would no sooner be cavalier with it than with my relationship with Mae.

I put my briefcase on the desk recently vacated by Cranmer, opened it, took out a can of Cinnaster I'd put there earlier, and marched to find the kitchen – which I had not yet fully inspected – and a freezer to quickly and properly chill the ale.

Stunned was too mild a word to explain my reaction to what I saw. This kitchen was state-of-the-art, not out of place in any five-star restaurant.

No 1970s-era avocado green or gold rusty refrigerators, no electric coil range like in my previous church kitchens. Instead, the commercial-grade galley at St. Aidan's sported a tall, white upright fridge and a stainless steel ten-burner gas range with dual ovens and a large copper vent hood above. I stood and gaped at all this, thinking the Macalesters must be in heaven here.

Then I noticed a hinged door with a silver handle. I pulled the handle and was greeted with a blast of frosty air and a bright bluish LED light. I entered the walk-in freezer, a space about seven-feet square with various victuals – mainly Ziploc bags full of fish – on shelves lining the freezer walls.

"This will do nicely," I thought, putting the can of Cinnaster on a wire shelf, exiting the freezer, reaching in my pocket for my phone, and setting the clock app timer for 20 minutes. I knew from experience that frozen beer is undrinkable, even after it unthaws.

I put the phone back in my pocket, exited the kitchen, and wended my way back to my office where a bottle of Pinot Grigio from what appeared to be a local vineyard rested on the polished mahogany desk. A small envelope was taped to the neck of the bottle, the note inside simply saying, "Welcome to St. Aidan's." I was not a huge wine drinker, but Mae would appreciate it.

On with the task at hand. I took my well-used Bible, Book of Common Prayer, and the blue 1982 hymnal out of the forementioned box, stacking them on the corner of the opulent desk. The new MacBook Pro 16-inch laptop resided on a pullout desk shelf. When I powered it on, it booted instantly.

The laptop battery had obviously been charged, probably by Dennis. The internet access at St. Aidan's, I'd learned, was provided through a local company that offered a reliable rural broadband service.

I clicked on the Safari browser icon and searched for the Episcopal lectionary page. When it came up, I added it to the bookmarks, then clicked on the link for next Sunday. My eyes were drawn to the Psalm for the day's first verse:

Behold, how good and how pleasant it is for brethren to dwell together in unity...

The perfect verse for an ecumenical congregation. No heavy doctrine involved.

I needed to make some notes before writing the sermon on the laptop. For certain tasks I preferred writing on paper instead of on a word processor, or worse, the even less-tangible "cloud." Call me old-fashioned, but I believe new is not necessarily better. I pulled out a yellow legal pad I'd placed earlier in the upper left desk drawer, and out of habit, reached for the Montblanc.

The only thing there was the holder. Hmmm. I was positive I'd put the pen there earlier.

This concerned me because I was always conscientious about not misplacing it because of Mae's thoughtfulness.

"Maybe whoever left the wine while I was in the kitchen used it to write the note and then absentmindedly slipped it into their pocket. Or maybe I'm just getting old and forgetful," I thought, the more likely scenario being my looming decrepitude and the busyness of setting up a new office. I'd probably slipped it into the middle desk drawer, but it wasn't there. I checked my shirt pocket, patting it like an absent-minded professor. It wasn't there, either.

I checked under and around the desk, even in the wastebasket, then went into the sanctuary thinking perhaps I had brought it to there to make note of a prayer request I'd received from a seminary classmate. I frantically checked the altar, the pulpit, the sacristy, even the acolyte robe closet, all without success.

As I stood in front of the altar, head down thinking about what I would tell Mae, my pocket vibrated and played a trumpet fanfare, warning me to retrieve my ale. I walked slowly to the kitchen, took the properly chilled Cinnaster from the freezer, carried it to my office, wiped the condensation off on my pant leg, and set the can on the desk mat far enough away from the laptop lest I clumsily spill beer on the keyboard. Then I leaned back in the hyper-comfortable high-back leather swivel chair and chalked up the missing writing utensil to creeping senility or whoever delivered the wine. I'd do a further search later, but for now I prayed for enlightenment concerning the pen and the sermon, pondered the words attributed to King David for a few minutes, then opened Microsoft Word and began to write.

Chapter 11

Friday afternoon Mae and I were listening to the local radio station – national news on the hour, local news following, weather on the 8s, ubiquitous conservative talk shows interspersed with home improvement and financial advice.

At 4:45, a steady stream of people began flowing past our window headed for the church and the weekly fish fry. "Well, let's do our duty and join in eating one of the things we know Jesus ate," I said to Mae, knowing fish wasn't her favorite, but hoping my reference to the Savior would ease her trepidation.

"If it's deep fried, I might have a nibble, but that's it. Maybe some cheeks," she said.

"Fair enough. Shall we head over?"

When we left our cabin arm in arm, I saw John and Belle Smyth, also arm in arm, walking slowly toward the kirk. Belle had a cane in her right hand.

We waited for them to make their way to us, then I said, "Well, good evening, Mr. and Mrs. Smyth. I pray all is well with you."

"And also with you," said John, greeting us with the all-purpose ecclesiastical greeting.

"This is my wife, Mae," I said to Belle, who smiled and said, "Nice to meet you, Mae. We'll have to get together for a talk soon."

"I'd like that," said Mae, looking forward to some female companionship, a thing not always easy to come by for a rector's wife.

When we reached the side door of the church granting access to the kitchen and dining hall, I held the door for the Smyths, then Mae and I entered and were greeted by Penny Burns.

"Good evening! So nice to see you Father you must be Mrs. MacManus." She took Mae's hand in both of hers. "I'm Penny Burns please come in and have a seat dinner will be served in just a few minutes Father you'll lead us in the table grace won't you?"

"Of course. Just let me know when."

"When the bell rings you pray sort of like a boxing match but without the punching," she giggled.

Before we found a chair at one of the round tables, we strolled past the serving line, already set with a large bowl of green salad followed by bottles of various dressings, then chafing trays filled with creamed corn, baked potatoes wrapped in tin foil, and finally two separate trays with fish – deep fried or broiled.

"Oh, good," whispered Mae. "I'll have the broiled."

"I thought you would," I said, knowing how fried foods disagreed with her digestion.

Malcolm Macalester stepped out of the kitchen and pulled the rope attached to the wall-mounted bell. The sound clanged loudly enough to get the attention of the 50 or so people waiting for dinner.

Penny stepped next to me, turned to the attendees, and said lustily, "Good evening, everyone so nice to see you here again for our first fantastic fabulous fish fry with our new priest Father MacManus here to lead us in prayer. Take it away, Father!"

Rather than speechify at this first group gathering, I simply said in my best preacher voice, "Let us pray." All present folded their hand, bowed their heads, and listened as I again quoted Robert Burns, who probably quoted someone else:

> *Some hae meat and canna eat,*
> *And some wad eat that want it,*
> *But we hae meat and we can eat,*
> *And sae the Lord be thankit.*

When nobody responded, I pronounced a loud and slow "Amen!"

A smattering of echoed Amens followed, after which Mae whispered to me, "I don't think they're used to 18th century poetry."

I whispered back, "Well, they'll learn."

As the diners filed through the line, filling their plates and taking them to tables, Penny Burns flitted about to help anyone who needed or didn't need assistance. I followed each to their tables and greeted them personally as a good priest should. Then Mae and I got in line in front of a tall, well-built fellow with a full beard turning gray and a full head of dark red hair. He wore a sleeveless T-shirt, his left upper arm bearing a "Semper Fi" tattoo. The expression on his face indicated he'd rather be anyplace else but here.

Before he could pick up a plate, Penny zipped over, grabbed my arm and said in her stream-of-consciousness way, "Father! Oh my gosh you haven't met my Harry yet this is Harry now that he's fully retired he'll be able to spend more time with me here on Bluestone. Harry this is our new priest, Father MacManus." Penny dashed back into the kitchen to help refill the chafing dishes, unnecessary since Harry was the last person served and the dishes still contained enough for seconds.

Harry and I shook hands, which I instantly regretted. His grip could have cracked a walnut. Thankfully, the shake didn't last long.

"Nice to meet you, Harry." I said, flexing my squashed fingers. Glancing at his arm, I said, "Am I correct in saying you served as a United States Marine?"

"The tattoo wouldn't be there if I hadn't," he said behind clenched teeth, his eyes and facial expression the epitome of an alpha male. Without another word, he picked up a plate and followed me to fill it with food.

Mae had been waiting patiently for me at a table with the Smyths and Tom Cooper. When I reached the end of the line, I noticed a basket overflowing with cash and checks, the free-will offering for tonight's meal. I put down my plate, reached into my pocket for my billfold only to see I had no cash. I'd become too used to using plastic.

My wallet back in place, I turned and noticed Penny, her hand on Tom Cooper's shoulder, leaning over him, smiling and chattering away. Her husband Harry sat by himself at a table in the back of the hall.

Thelma Wadewitz and Millie TerHorst sat together while the rest of the tables were taken with other island residents and people I hadn't met, some perhaps relatives or friends of Bluestone Island residents or townies.

Mae and I had a pleasant evening dining and visiting with Tom and the Smyths. A priest should not have favorites, but I already felt a professional bond with John, and Tom needed someone to share his heartache.

As the crowd dispersed and we said our farewells, Thelma could be heard practicing "Jesu, Joy of Man's Desiring" exceedingly loudly and slowly.

I could hear J. S. Bach snoring in his grave.

Chapter 12

St. Aidan's, festooned in toilet paper, looked almost jubilant as I approached the kirk the second to the last Sunday in May a full hour before the service. Whoever did this must have had arms belonging in major league baseball.

No time to tidy up, and even if there were time, maybe I could work this "artistry" into the homily or at least the announcements.

I pulled the red door open to the narthex/foyer, flipped on the bank of light switches, and walked down the main aisle, appreciating the splendor of this island church, the morning light streaming through the stained-glass, Charmin-filtered windows. I stood in front of the altar and prayed for courage and enlightenment to lead the service.

"Well, they've done it again," Thelma Wadewitz howled from the bottom of the chancel steps. I'd been so absorbed in prayer I didn't hear her enter. I turned to see her standing there, an old, beat-up briefcase dangling from her right hand, evidently the repository for her music.

By now I was used to standing close to Thelma and speaking slowly and loudly. I stepped down next to her and said, "WHO HAS DONE IT AGAIN?"

"Those hooligans from town. Every spring it's the same thing."

Remembering my younger days, thinking the hooligans were probably high school seniors having a literal TP fling before graduation. They could have done worse than creating a nuisance.

"Well, I better get on with it," said Thelma, floating over to the organ bench, belying her age like when I first saw her working at her flower bed. She plopped her briefcase on the organ bench, snapped open the catch, took out a tattered score, put it on the music rack, turned on the instrument, and begin to play.

Loudly. And slowly.

I left Thelma to her pre-service practice routine and snuck to my office for more prayer, especially for the music ministry at St.

Aidan's, and to look over my sermon. At ten minutes before mass would begin, I could hear people talking loudly in the narthex and others in more subdued tones in the sanctuary. At least some still observed proper respect for sacred space.

I quickly went to the sacristy to don my vestments, green during this liturgical season, and met Malcolm Macalester.

"Good morning, Malcolm." He was struggling into the white robe acolytes and other assistants wore at Episcopal and other liturgical churches. Cranmer sat in the corner, staring indifferently at Malcolm's problem.

"Good morning, Father. Might I ask for a little help? It seems I've gained some weight since I served as crucifer last summer."

"A man of your culinary artistry is certainly allowed a few extra pounds," I said, lifting the robe's shoulders as he slipped his arms in the sleeves. Once we were both suitably attired, Malcolm lifted the processional cross from its stand and we both departed for the back of the nave/church proper as Thelma finished her prelude. It sounded like something by the French composer Cesar Franck, but with Thelma (and Franck), you could never tell.

We waited an inordinately long time for Thelma to introduce the processional hymn. It appeared she had dropped her playing glasses on the organ's pedal board, and was on her hands and knees like a nearsighted spaniel, contorting herself to reach the tortoise shell framed spectacles which, of course, had fallen in the most inconvenient spot. Finally, Mae got up from her pew and helped Thelma recover her glasses, if not her dignity.

At last Thelma intoned a short introduction to "Holy, Holy, Holy, Lord God Almighty," which the congregation, in good Episcopal fashion – juggling the pew bulletin containing the order of service, hymnal, and Book of Common Prayer – sang in good spirit, if not in good tune, tempo, and rhythm.

Malcolm and I processed, attempting to sing along with Thelma, who had the organ at full volume, so full that nobody could hear anything else. The hymn should have taken two minutes, but instead took nearly four.

Malcolm stood behind the lectern as I stood in the center of the chancel and said, just as Cranmer entered from the sacristy and stood to my right, surveying the congregation:

"Almighty God, to you all hearts are open, all desires known, and from you no secrets are hid: Cleanse the thoughts of our hearts by the inspiration of your Holy Spirit, that we may perfectly love you, and worthily magnify your holy Name; through Christ our Lord."

The congregation responded with a hearty Amen, and mass began.

+ + +

The service went relatively well. Malcolm read the lessons and led the prayers of the people with full, confident voice. My sermon text, oddly or God-inspired, was taken from another psalm, instead of the one I'd read earlier in the week.

"Remember not the sins of my youth," which might seem an odd text to preach to a congregation of retirees, but then again, why not? Who hasn't done or said things when young that we wish we could take back? Besides, who am I to argue with the Holy Spirit? It also gave me a chance to put my tongue in my cheek and nod to the toilet paper hanging behind the stained glass. I smiled and surveyed the faithful. Most smiled or chuckled in return.

Millie TerHorst, however, did not. Her expression resembled a redundant yet appropriate shriveled prune, especially when she looked at Cranmer, who had curled up on Belle Smyth's lap.

After the sermon, prayers, and passing of the peace, I stood by the first pew and said, "I want to thank you all for making Mae and me feel welcome at St. Aidan's. I'm sure we will all be a blessing to each other this summer and many summers to come." Millie's expression, if anything, was still more sour than a wrinkled lemon.

"After coffee following mass, I would like to see the vestry for a very short meeting in the conference room." I emphasized *very short*, remembering some of the knock-down, drag-outs at St. Andrew's that went far into the evening.

+ + +

Once coffee time wound down, the vestry and I, five in number, found our way to the conference room. Not surprisingly, Millie asserted herself before I had the chance to mention my brief agenda, the only item being the publication of a small congregational pictorial directory.

"I demand something be done about these hoodlums. The display this morning is nothing less than scandalous."

"I assume you're referring to the beauteous white streamers adorning our building," I said, trying to lighten Millie's mood. I should have known better. Lightening Millie TerHorst's mood was like forcing deodorant on a skunk.

"To be on the safe side, we might consider locking the doors," said Dennis, "although that goes against tradition and history of the church being a sanctuary and wouldn't solve the toilet paper problem."

"Those ne'er-do-wells don't need sanctuary, although the doors absolutely need to be locked. Those criminals need to be tossed in the clink," said Millie. "Every place in town has those spy cameras now. Why don't we? Then we could see the perps and bring them to justice."

Millie's obviously been watching too much crime TV. I looked at Dennis to get his take.

He thought for a moment and said, "The spy cameras, as Millie calls them, are quite inexpensive. The work would be in wiring them to a hard drive capturing the activity. I'd suggest, since Father is here most often, routing the feed to his computer. He could then check it as necessary and report any suspicious activity to the authorities. Right now, the activity seems to me an inconvenience."

"Call it what you will," sneered Millie. "It's a poke in the eye of the church, this annual custom for these … these … criminals. We have to do something before they burn the church to the ground!" She folded her arms across her chest and glared at me, like it was my idea to TP the church.

"So, this has happened before?" I asked.

"Every spring since I've been on the island," said John Smyth. "I actually think it's kind of pretty, but I know it inconveniences Dennis and whoever helps clean it up."

"Actually, Millie has a point," said Dennis. "It seems that for the last few years, the 'criminals' have become bolder, entering the building and pilfering the communion wine and spreading flour and Fiona's spices around the kitchen, even getting into the freezer and tossing packages of frozen fish around, although not last night, thanks be to God. Our doors have always been unlocked, but maybe the time has come to revisit that tradition."

I could see my questions about the church directory would have to wait for next month.

"If you like, I can look into security cameras and report back," said Dennis.

"I move that the church doors be locked from dusk 'til dawn, or at least install locks on the kitchen freezer and spice drawers, and that Dennis O'Neill be given permission to purchase spy cameras as soon as possible," said Millie, standing to emphasis her motion. "And I will pay for them." She glared at us, daring anyone to disagree.

"I second the motion regarding the cameras and locks in the kitchen, but move to delay discussion on locking the church doors," said John.

"Do we need a vote, or are we all agreed?" said Dennis. As the only warden of this small community, he didn't stand on ceremony. "Anyone opposed to Millie and John's motions?"

Millie sneered, "Why in the name of John Knox would anyone be opposed?"

Nobody dared.

Chapter 13

I dressed in my black clergy shirt, matching pants, dog collar, and a gray sport coat again against the spring chill on my morning walk around the island Tuesday morning when Dennis pulled up to the communal dock in his bass boat. He and Harry Burns – mostly Harry – supply the fish for the Friday fries. In order to stay on the right side of the law, they never kept more fish than were needed for that week's feast. Jesus would be pleased since He taught us to ask for *daily* bread. I was certain He would allow weekly fish as well.

I stood and waited for Dennis, who sported a green flannel shirt, well-worn jeans, and work boots, to tie off at the communal dock. His baseball cap advertised what I assumed was fishing gear. I watched him as he clambered out of his boat with a box under his arm.

"Father, I have to tell you this is going to be way simpler than I expected," he said, lifting the box a few inches. Having been lost in contemplation of next Sunday's gospel, I blinked at him and furrowed my brow.

"When I went home Sunday after the vestry meeting, I got on the computer, hopped on Amazon, did a little research, and ordered Millie's security system. Since Trudy has Amazon Prime, it arrived yesterday afternoon. Can we go to your office so I can show it to you?" He was talking like a kid with a new set of Legos.

"Certainly," I said, as we walked together up the path to the church, the box with the ubiquitous smiley logo in his hands.

"I could hardly believe how easy installing this system will be," he said, placing the opened box on my desk. "The best part is, it's wireless and solar powered, so no batteries ever need to be replaced, and it will run on the same system your computer's wireless internet uses. And it's also night-vision capable, so I suggest positioning one of the three cameras pointing to the front door, one in the kitchen, and one at the back entrance. More cameras can be added if necessary, and in the fall, we simply take down the outdoor cameras from their roosts in the trees and store them until next spring. Easy-peasy, lemon-squeezy, as my grandkids say."

"Wait a minute," I said. "If I'm responsible for monitoring this, does that mean I will have to watch hours of what three cameras capture every day?" If this is ministry in the modern era, I was already looking for a way to delegate this responsibility.

"Not at all," said Dennis, shaking his capped head. "I read the whole instruction book last night. The beauty of this system is that it's motion sensitive. The only time the cameras will capture a scene to your computer is when something moves, triggering the system. Then it goes dormant once the motion stops. Software on your computer then alerts you so you can take a look at only the cameras that were activated for the time motion was detected. And you can disable any section of the system at any time, like the kitchen camera on Friday nights when only Fiona and Malcolm are there."

"Well, that seems simple enough," I said, reminding myself to disable the kitchen camera on Friday nights, although I doubted I'd remember. I was still skeptical and thought of handing off this obligation, but I hadn't been here long enough to cause waves. I'd learned long ago which battles to fight and which to surrender. Besides, Dennis had been a good and helpful warden. I didn't want to fight him on this. Besides, the vestry had approved it at Millie's insistence.

Dennis unpacked the cameras. They looked like black boxes not much bigger than fair-sized novels. Each had two vertical eyes, the top one a little larger than the bottom, and two pointy antennas the size of pencils laid back like a bloodhound's ears in full chase mode.

"I can have these in place and the software installed on your laptop by this afternoon," said Dennis. "Then a test of the system and we should be set."

I've never, ever seen anything move this fast in any of the other parishes I'd served, but I suppose smaller congregations like St.

Aidan's can move more quickly than larger urban parishes where every decision had to be filtered through several committees. I agreed to Dennis's plan, but then asked, "How much will this set Millie back?" I didn't need her complaining, although she did say she'd cover the cost.

Dennis smiled wickedly at me and said, "About the same as four bottles of Jameson's."

Knowing that one bottle of this fine Irish whiskey only costs about the price of a full tank of gas in a mid-sized car, I said, "Well, then. I don't think Millie will mind, but let's keep the cost comparison between us."

+ + +

Since Dennis would be busy installing cameras around the property and software on my office laptop, I walked the rest of the island's circumference, thinking about toilet paper, a floured kitchen, time-honored sanctuary practices, communion wine, and Millie. I supposed installing the security system was the prudent thing, but surely the church's insurance policy would cover any real damage. Tempest in a teapot, I thought.

After the cameras show nothing more than a curious raccoon at the back door, all will be forgotten until next spring when the graduating seniors at Bluestone High show up with another case of Charmin. Even if the cameras could identify those involved, there was no way I would support prosecuting them, Millie's insistence notwithstanding. Simply locking the doors, which I imagine might someday be added to my daily tasks, would solve the other problems, although that had not been voted on and I hoped it would not.

I went back to our cabin and spent the rest of the morning at the dining table reading the *Bluestone Gazette* someone had graciously left on our doorstep. Mae, unencumbered from her usual summer preparations for the coming school year, cozied herself on the couch reading an Amish novel, Cranmer curled up next to her.

"So, you and the cat ... " I said.

"Yes," said Mae, rubbing her hand over Cranmer's back. "He seems to have taken a liking to me. Comes meowing at the door when you're gone."

"Well, as long as he doesn't scratch the furniture to shreds."

Mae informed me the Yoder family in her book struggled with their teenage daughter wanting to sample the "Englisher" life. Our radio and Cranmer's purring supplied soft background as I looked at the religion page that consisted solely of worship times at local churches, St. Aidan's 9:30 time included. St. Joseph's Catholic offered mass Saturday evening at 6:00 and Sunday morning at 10:30. The three Lutheran churches of varying denominational flavors met earlier on Sunday mornings than St. Joseph's or St. Aidan's.

We had a leisurely lunch of turkey sandwiches on cracked wheat bread, string cheese, strawberries, and sparkling water, all of which my lovely wife had procured on her now weekly delivery from the Pick-Em Up she'd scheduled with Shorty Dvorak.

At 1:30, I said, "Time to get back to work. Dennis said he'd have the security system up and running by this afternoon."

"That whole thing makes me uneasy," said Mae, clearing the table. "Too many unknowns. What if these cameras caught a parishioner committing an illegal act? Would you be legally bound to report them to the authorities? What about people coming to you for counseling? There are privacy issues here."

"I assure you, no camera will show any part of my office at any time, especially if I were I to be counseling anyone, and as far as illegal acts, what might they be? Pilfering an extra donut during coffee hour?"

"You never know," said Mae. "That's what 'unknowns' means."

Chapter 14

Dennis sat staring at my laptop's display, mouse in hand.

"This is the coolest thing since automatic transmissions," he said. "Come take a look."

Dennis got out of my chair and motioned for me to take a seat. The computer screen was divided into four quadrants, one being gray, the others showing the areas monitored by the three cameras. Dennis has evidently set the cameras to show the three areas without motion activation.

"Impressive," I said, and meant it. The clarity of the shots was as good as any high-definition television, but I was still leery of the whole project. I'd never fancied myself a spy.

"This system has a zoom feature. Let me show you." He moved behind me, clicked the mouse on the kitchen quadrant. He pulled his finger over the mouse's roller, and focused in on the sink's faucet.

"That is amazing," I said. "What can technology not do?"

"Some churches broadcast their services using a system very much like this," said Dennis.

"That's where I draw the line," I said. "There's still much to be said about human contact. For the church to be what it should be, we need to be able to talk to one another face to face, to shake hands, to look into each other's eyes ... "

"I get it," said Dennis. "Just a modern possibility. One of the Lutheran churches in town live-streams their services. The shut-ins love it."

"Well, when St. Aidan's has shut-ins, I'll consider it. Until then, no cameras in the sanctuary."

"Let me reset the system and then we'll run a live check," said Dennis, reaching for the mouse and setting the camera display back to its original setting. "I'll head for the kitchen and you watch the monitor," he said. With that he loped out of my office while I stared at the laptop. In thirty seconds, a small green light flashed at the bottom of the screen and the kitchen quadrant appeared, revealing my warden grinning at the camera, waving his arms. Then he left, and in a few moments the green light flashed again and Dennis appeared at the quadrant showing the back door. A few more moments and he appeared at the third, front door quadrant, pretending to reel in a lunker walleye from the lake. In another thirty seconds he was back in my office.

"Well, what do you think?" he said.

"You showed up as clear as a crystal goblet filled with spring water on all three cameras."

He clapped his hands and said, "Now we show it to the vestry next Sunday."

There went my church picture directory plans again.

+ + +

As Dennis stood to leave my office, another face appeared at my door.

"Knock, knock," said Ingrid Larssen, her smile brighter than a summer sunrise. She hugged a three-ring binder to her with both arms and said, "Good afternoon, Mr. O'Neill. Nice to see you as always."

"Right back at'cha, Ingrid. I'd love to stay and chat, but that front door won't fix itself." Dennis nodded to Ingrid and stepped around her to his weekly effort of keeping mice out of the sanctuary.

"To what do I owe this pleasure?" I said, standing and smiling at Ingrid in all her Scandinavian wholesomeness.

"Tuesday is my least favorite, but totally necessary day, Father. I'm here to collect for last week's groceries."

"Ah, yes. Now I recall," I said, remembering that the Pick-Em-Up simply ran a tab for island residents, knowing that if anyone welshed on a debt, the church would cover it, then get reimbursed by the welsher. "Please go see my wife. She holds the purse strings in the family. Do you know which cabin is ours?"

"Yes. Right next to Millie."

"Yes indeed," I said. "How are your career plans shaping up?"

"Right on track. Next year at this time I should be at our store in Alexandria. I'm a little nervous, but looking forward to it."

I couldn't help thinking that with her intelligence and looks, Ingrid could be looking for something more out of life, but then again, I was assuming, not to mention profiling. There's absolutely nothing wrong with a young woman managing a grocery store.

"I better be on my way then," said Ingrid. "I like to finish my Tuesday rounds by 3:00, but some of our customers like to talk. I don't like to cut them short, but sometimes I have to delicately extricate myself from a conversation or I wouldn't get back for the late afternoon rush."

"I totally understand," I said, recalling the many times parishioners would bend my ear for what seemed like an eternity. But then, listening was a large part of a priest's call. It wasn't Ingrid's. Her call was business.

"Stop and see my wife and she'll settle up with you. Godspeed on your duties."

"Thanks, Father." Ingrid turned and bounced out of my office.

I wondered how long Penny would keep her as I sat at my desk thinking thought about "spy cameras." I took a standard #2 pencil out of the middle desk drawer, and wrote on my yellow legal pad:

Technology is a marvel;
It can do so much good,
But just because we can do something
Doesn't mean that we should.

Chapter 15

Wednesday nights at St. Aidan's were wonderfully free of the usual business of board meetings and the other church necessities at my previous parishes, so Mae and I took midweek nights as our together time. Since the weather was turning phenomenally pleasant, we either strolled the island or, like this evening, sat on the Adirondack chairs on our T-shaped dock – the only stand-alone dock on the island due to my "exalted" position – holding hands and staring over the water, enjoying one another's company.

"Aren't you terribly bored stuck in the cabin all day while I gallivant around the island or spend inordinate amounts of time at the church?"

"Not at all," said Mae. "Since I no longer have papers to grade, lesson plans to write, or planning for the fall term, I finally have time for myself. I should have told you that was one of the reasons I hoped you would accept this position. Is that terribly selfish of me?"

"Absolutely not," I said. "Most people don't realize the burden a clergyman's wife carries, especially one with a more than full-time job, not to mention parishioners watching her every move and critiquing her hair and clothing."

"And also riding herd on her husband so he doesn't work himself into a divorce."

I dropped her hand, turned to her and said, serious as a heart attack, "Have you actually considered it?" I thought back to our time at St. Andrew's and the burdens that parish laid on its priests resulting in them not staying for more than a few years.

"Not seriously," she said.

"But you did think about it."

"Only when I felt ignored, lonely, or forgotten. I knew what I'd signed up for when we married. Thank God for some of the other wives in the diocese. Misery loved company."

I took her hand again and said, "You've been a trooper. That's one of the things I love about you. When I retire and you'll be so un-ignored, un-lonely, and un-forgotten that you'll want to chuck me off this dock."

She squeezed my hand and said, "We'll see about that. Since we've made it this far, we should probably stick it out to the bitter end." Then she turned to me and smiled her enigmatic smile. Mona Lisa has nothing on Mae Carson-MacManus.

We leaned back and looked out over the placid evening water, a boat slowly trolling about 75 meters to our left with a lone fisherman's line in the water.

"There's Harry Burns, catching our Friday night meal," I said. "That beard and hair give him away even from this distance. Did you meet him last week?"

"I saw him sitting by himself at the fish fry while Penny worked the room. He didn't look too happy."

"Maybe he's just introverted. Could be the old opposites attract theory."

"When I tried to draw him into a conversation, all I got was grunts and head shakes and nods," Mae whispered, knowing that sounds carry over water. "I get the feeling there's more than introversion going on."

"Yes, it could be depression, but I need to know him better before making assumptions."

Just then Harry cut his motor and began reeling in earnest, finally netting what appeared to be a good-sized walleye. He unhooked the fish, dropped it into the boat's live well, rebaited his hook, turned his silent electric motor back on, cast his line back in the water, and trolled on. When he got even with our dock, I yelled, "Hullo, Harry! How goes the catch?"

He turned his head and glowered at us for five seconds, turned to look over his shoulder, then started his inboard motor and sped off, leaving us wondering what was eating Harry Burns.

+ + +

"Let's head on in," said Mae. "Downton Abbey is coming on in about ten minutes."

Far be it from me to stand between my wife and her favorite British drama, so we unwound ourselves from our chairs in the gloaming and stepped single file off the dock to our cabin. Before we opened the door, the sound of bagpipe drones drifted over us followed by the sad old Scottish folk song, "Flowers of the Forest."

"Good Lord, I haven't heard that song since my grandfather's funeral," I said. We stood at attention at our front door as a modern translation played in my mind:

I've seen the smiling of fortune beguiling,
I've tasted her pleasures and felt her decay;
Sweet is her blessing, and kind her caressing,
But now they are fled and fled far away.

I reached for Mae's hand as we listened to the pipes reprise the tune. Suddenly the temperature dropped twenty degrees and what was left of the evening light vanished behind a bank of coal-black clouds.

Chapter 16

The pop-up thunderstorm last night washed the island, leaving everything smelling new and fresh this Thursday morning. I was not ready to shut myself into my office and compose this week's sermon, so I left home, turned left, and headed for Harry's cabin. Something was bothering him, and as his spiritual guide, I felt it my place to try and find out what it was through simple conversation.

A radio behind the Burns's cabin played the local country station, so I took it upon myself to investigate. When I reached the cabin's corner, I saw Harry burying the remains of last night's catch under a willow tree.

"Hullo, Harry! Looks like you had a successful trip," I said, standing a respectful distance away.

He glanced over at me and said, "It's easy if you know where they are," wiping his hands on an old rag.

"So do you have one of those fancy fish finders?" I said.

He almost smiled, but then simply pointed to his head.

"Ah, a fellow old-fashioned soul," I said. "I spent most of my life hacking away on an old Underwood typewriter. I'm still trying to wrap my head around the new computer in my office."

He perked up and said, "What kind is it?"

"I think it's an Apple," I fibbed, knowing full well it was a MacBook Pro. "About the only thing I know is how to turn it on and find the word processor," which was mostly true.

Harry lay the filthy rag on his fish cleaning table next to a can of Schell's beer – a Minnesota brand similar to what Budweiser is to Missouri, only on a smaller scale – and said, "Mind if I take a look?"

I noticed several empty, crushed beer cans on Harry's table. "I'd be thrilled for you to look at the laptop. I was just about to head to the office and work on Sunday's sermon. Would you have time this morning? I could sure use some tips on how to use the internet."

OK, I knew how to use the Internet and handle e-mails, but I was sure I didn't know everything.

"Give me about fifteen minutes to get these filets in Baggies. I'll meet you there," he said.

+ + +

I knew from previous discussion with Penny that Harry had worked for an on-line company, so this connection worked to my advantage. Now that the ice had been broken, perhaps Harry would open up to me. I had to remind myself to take it slow, lest I spoil the chance to minister to him.

True to his word, Harry showed up at my office door carrying a pail that contained the recently caught fish neatly packaged in plastic bags. "Let me get these in the freezer and I'll be right back," he said. I looked up from behind the computer, smiled, and watched him depart for the kitchen. When he returned, I was two-fingering it through my sermon's introductory paragraph. He stood in the doorway until I invited him in.

"Harry, please come in and have a look at this beast," I said. "Beast" was not really appropriate concerning earlier, slow desktop monsters I'd worked on previously. This laptop was sleek and speedy, as different from my old Underwood as Minnesota from Mexico.

I got up and out of my chair, motioning for Harry to take my place. He seemed hesitant, but sat, looked at the laptop, and said, "What do you want to know?"

Just the opening I was hoping for, so I said, "We've had this security system set up with three cameras patrolling the front and back of the church as well as the kitchen." I told him how the cameras only activate when motion is detected, and how each of the three areas can be disabled, and the lights that show when motion has been detected.

"Pretty simple stuff," said Harry.

"Simple for you," I said, "but I feel a bit like a voyeur reviewing these videos." Then I took the plunge. "Would you consider coming in, maybe on Tuesdays just to review the activity?" I gave him my best puppy-dog look.

He looked at me, his hands folded and said, "Sorry, but I don't think so."

Rats. "Well, if I ever have questions about the computer, can I count on your help?"

"Sure," said Harry. He got up and said, "Excuse me, but I need to hose down my fish cleaning station before that damn...er...dang cat gets at it again."

"Certainly, I said," stepping aside, thinking about small steps.

Chapter 17

Thelma's rendition of "Jerusalem" by Sir Hubert Parry, suitably lethargic, led the procession down the aisle the last Sunday in May. John Smyth, clothed in a classic white alb/robe, held the processional cross high, followed this Sunday by the similarly properly-robed Malcolm Macalester, then me in my green chasuble, adding a splash of color to the procession and identifying me as clergy to anyone in question.

When Thelma informed me on Tuesday what she would play for the prelude on Sunday, I told her we would not need an entrance hymn (much to her dismay) because any music following that stirring tune would be anticlimactic.

The unofficial anthem of Scotland, "Flowers of Scotland," is held in high regard, but Alba (the Gaelic name for the land), being still a tenuous member of the United Kingdom, also claims Parry's tune married to a poem by William Blake. "Jerusalem," alongside "God Save the King," are the unofficial anthems of the UK. Parry's tune stirs even American hearts.

As we processed, the words of Blake's poem ran through my consciousness:

> *And did those feet in ancient time,*
> *Walk upon England's mountains green;*
> *And was the holy Lamb of God,*
> *On England's pleasant pastures seen?*

Once we were in place and waiting for Thelma to finish, I readied myself front and center, then began:

"Bless the Lord who forgives all our sins," to which the people responded, *"His mercy endures for ever."*

Cranmer, standing behind the organ bench, responded with a menacing growl. Thelma turned and said in a stage whisper loud enough for everyone this side of the Mississippi River to hear, "Shoo! Shoo!" waving her right hand like she was swatting flies.

Cranmer simply stalked off and jumped up on the pew next to Belle Smyth, who reached over and scratched his ear while I went on with the collect for purity:

"Almighty God, to you all hearts are open, all desires known, and from you no secrets are hid ..."

The service continued apace, Malcolm reading the lessons, Thelma leading us through the Gradual hymn, I sermonizing in what I considered a lesser but tolerable effort. John led the prayers of the people in what I imagined the voice of God to be like.

During the distribution of the sacrament, I handed the bread to my congregants while John followed with the chalice of wine. I realized how each member in their own way contributed to the family at St. Aidan's: Fiona with her culinary and musical skills; Tom with his calm demeanor; Millie and her almost military philosophy of life; Mae with her constant support; Penny with her servant heart; even Cranmer, who followed Belle to the altar rail and sat next to her as she stood, choosing not to kneel to receive the bread and wine due to her arthritic knees and hips.

Immediately following the final blessing, I made the following announcement:

"On next Friday, the first Friday evening in June, in lieu of Malcolm and Fiona's absence to Minneapolis, you are all invited to a pot-luck barbecue at the rector's cabin. Mae and I will provide burgers, hot dogs, table service, and other necessary accompaniments. Please bring a dish to share, folding chairs if you have them, and your favorite beverage. Also, please RSVP by calling or e-mailing the church by Wednesday."

After my announcement, I said, "The mass is ended. Go in peace to love and serve the Lord."

I stood behind Thelma, greeting the exiting congregants while she blared a postlude that may have been a 19th century English voluntary or an improvisation on "How Much Is That Doggie in the Window?"

+   +   +

At coffee hour after mass, Penny carried her cup around the Fellowship Hall bending any and all ears. "I had a terrible time getting to sleep again Wednesday night did you sleep well some huge bird squawked loud enough to wake the dead I hope it flies away chop-chop ..." She carried on to whoever would listen until finally John Smyth took her aside.

"Penny, you're new to the island. What you heard was no bird. You heard Fiona's bagpipes. She's gotten quite a following from the islanders and the town for her thrilling Wednesday night recitals."

"Well, it sounded like a bird to me maybe a goose or a guinea hen they are terrible birds just as soon bite your toes off as look at you. My uncle had a whole flock of them and I stayed away because they were so aggressive they practically scared me to death chasing me around the barnyard and loud? You never heard such a racket ..."

Fiona had left the kitchen to refill the coffee pots and heard Penny's whole tirade equating her piping to a goose. When Penny noticed Fiona scowling at her, she turned to her and said, "I didn't mean *you* were a bird, Fiona, I just said you *sounded* like a big noisy bird ..."

John cleared his throat, lightly took Penny's arm, turned her away from Fiona lest the situation devolve into a catfight, and said in the kindest way, "In any case, Penny, I hope you'll be a good sport and realize that what annoys you can bring other people joy."

"Oh well if she plays every Wednesday night maybe I'll just turn up the TV have you ever seen CSI they almost always solve the crime …"

I said a silent prayer of thanks for John's intervention with Penny. Maybe this week's homily will mention fulfilling the law of Christ by bearing one another's burdens. John Smyth certainly bore mine this morning.

Harry Burns, who had not been present for the service or coffee hour, stood in the fellowship hall doorway waiting for his wife. Penny had sauntered over to Tom Cooper, talking her blue streak. Once Tom had detached himself from Penny and struck up a conversation with Dennis O'Neill, Harry, looking none too pleased, escorted Penny out of the building.

Chapter 18

On the first Tuesday morning in June, Penny appeared at my office door, arms full of mail.

"Here's your mail Father I hope you don't mind but I always read the front page of your Gazette just trying to keep up with current events around town isn't it something what goes on in this state not to mention the world why if someone doesn't do something soon …"

I waited for her to take a breath, then before she could get her second wind, said, "Penny, by any chance did you borrow my pen when you delivered the mail at some point?" I motioned to the empty pen stand on the top right corner of the desk pad.

"Oh no Father I never touch anything on your desk beside brushing my knuckles on it when I put your mail on the corner like this by the way you sure get a ton of junk mail just like everyone else on the island isn't there someplace you can write to stop that like the no-call feature on the phone …"

While she went on about spam calls and whatever else entered her consciousness, I tried to be a good priest, and listened until my eyes glazed over. When she at last talked herself out and left, I went through the mail, putting several music publisher ads in Thelma's workroom mailbox and then laid several letters of financial interest on Maureen's disk. I'd decided long ago to stay as far away from the financial aspects of my parishes as possible. I'd known priests who had gotten into trouble trying to be their congregation's Chief Financial Officer. One was serving time in the Massachusetts Correctional Institution for embezzlement to cover her gambling debts.

I recycled the rest of the mail except for a letter from my alma mater. Interesting how institutions keep their mailing lists up to date, almost always in an effort to solicit funds for one project or another.

I sighed and opened the middle desk drawer to find my letter opener missing.

+ + +

A light rap on our door interrupted Tuesday lunch with Mae. I got up to answer it and saw Ingrid Larssen smiling at me, holding an old-fashioned receipt book.

"Hello, Father. Is your wife here?"

"Of course, Ingrid," I said, happy to see the upbeat young woman again. "Please come in. Have you had lunch?"

"Yes, I'm fine," said Ingrid. "I've come to collect your grocery bill again." She flipped through the ledger, looking for our bill. "Your total comes to $176.49. Like last time, you may pay by cash, check, or credit card." She pulled a cell phone with a small attached card reader out of her back jeans pocket.

I felt Mae standing at my shoulder. I said, "Mae, do you remember Ingrid?"

"Absolutely," said Mae. "Hello, Ingrid. Is it collection day again?"

"Yes, ma'am. Time certainly flies."

"Let me get our checkbook," said Mae, scurrying to find her purse in our bedroom.

"So, Ingrid," I said, "is your career path on track? I seem to remember your father is prepping you for a management position."

"Yes," she smiled. "As I mentioned earlier, I'll be the assistant manager at our store in Alexandria starting this fall. It'll be my first time away from home, except for college, but I'm excited for the opportunity."

I recalled having this very discussion the last time I saw Ingrid. I needed to expand my repertoire. "You'll do just fine," I said, giving her my best encouraging smile.

"What do we owe you?" said Mae, back with checkbook in hand. We had opened an account at the local branch of Wells Fargo the week we arrived. Maureen had set my generous salary up to be automatically deposited from the church coffers.

Checking her ledger again, Ingrid said, "$176.49."

Mae used my shoulders as a desk, wrote out the check, tore it out of the book, and handed it to Ingrid.

"There you go, dear," said Mae.

Ingrid marked our bill paid and handed a carbon copy to Mae, saying, "Thank you for your business. See you in two weeks." She turned to head to her next stop, but stopped and said to me, "I sang in the choir at St. Olaf. My church in town does not have a music program in the summer. Might you have use of a soloist at St. Aidan's sometime? I'd love to stay in practice."

"From what I've seen here, our music ministry is quite small," thinking of Thelma. "But yes, I can certainly find a place for you to offer your talent."

"Please let me know," said Ingrid. "Call or e-mail me at the store anytime." Then she smiled, turned, and went on her way.

"What a nice young woman," said Mae.

+ + +

That night I realized I could not remember ever sleeping as well as I do here on the island. The sound of the wind through the trees, the lapping of water on the shore, and the plaintive cry of loons washed the cares of the day away. My evening prayer at bedtime rarely ended before my eyes shut and I fell asleep before hearing Mae's gentle whistling snores.

Chapter 19

"Now is the month of Maying when merry lads are playing ..."

I've been known to break out in song from time to time, and the glorious weather the last week in May and early June brought to mind a madrigal I'd learned in my high school choir containing a homophone of my good wife's name. The 16th century composer, Thomas Morley, would be pleased I could still hold my own on the bass line.

... Fa la la la la la la, lalala, Fa la la la la la laaa ...

Mae ignored my warbling, content to sip her herbal chamomile tea and gaze over Bluestone Lake from her dock chair this Wednesday evening. Her legs were crossed at the knee, her ankles absentmindedly flipping her tan flip-flops. She had the beginnings of a nice tan on her thighs from her days reading on a chaise longue on our front porch. Tonight, she had the appearance of a tabloid queen with oversized mirrored sunglasses and floppy sun hat. She flopped from head to toe.

"Don't you know any other obscure Renaissance pieces?" she asked between sips.

"I know a few, but none as appropriate, calendar-wise," I said.

"I dread hearing you croon a more time-appropriate June-moon-spoon tune."

"I don't know of such, but I can write one," I said, warming to the challenge.

"Don't forget to include a loon," she said. "It's the state bird."

I sat back, my ankles crossed, head tipped back, face absorbing the waning rays of the evening sun, when I noticed Harry Burns's boat approaching from the east, trolling slowly and silently, propelled by his electric motor. If I'd had my eyes closed, I would not even have noticed him except for Penny in the boats bow, leaning towards Harry and talking in what appeared to be serious but somber manner.

As they approached our dock, Harry shushed Penny and looked toward us. Penny turned, saw us, then turned back to Harry with no comment or wave. Harry started his motor and buzzed around the island to their dock and cabin.

"Interesting," said Mae.

"Indeed," I said.

"Will you investigate?" said Mae.

"No. They both saw us. If they want to explain, I'll listen, but I won't pry."

Heading toward 9:00 p.m., the sun continued its daily trip to the west. The air cooled enough to get us out of our chairs and headed back inside for the night, but not before we heard Fiona and her pipes break out in a thrilling rendition of "Scotland the Brave."

"If that doesn't get every Scot's blood rushing, nothing will," I said.

"Oh, simmer down and let's get inside," said Mae. Then she looked at me out of the corner of her eye, smiled, and said, "You can simmer up once we get ready for bed."

"Yes, ma'am," I said, taking her hand and pulling her off the deck and into the cabin.

Chapter 20

Prayer at the altar was always necessary before tackling my daily tasks. After conversing with the Almighty, I pushed myself up from the altar rail at 8:30 sharp Thursday morning and headed for my office, hearing the ring tone of the office phone.

"Good morning. St. Aidan's-on-the-Lake Episcopal Church. Father MacManus speaking. How may I help you?" as I sidled behind the desk and sunk into the luxury of the leather chair.

"And a good morning to you, Angus. I called to ask the same question."

I was temporarily taken aback until I recognized the voice.

"Good morning, bishop Farley! To what do I owe this virtual visit?"

"First off, it's Bob. Save the formality when you speak of me to your flock. How are things going at your island cathedral?"

"Quite well, thank you. Getting oriented, visiting the inhabitants, trying to get my office functional, working on my workflow; the usual activities."

"Very good. I assume you received our little welcome gift."

"So, the wine came from you?"

"Yes. We – that is, the staff here – always enjoys welcoming our new priests with a nice bottle of our Lord's unblessed blood."

"Mae and I will enjoy it, although I doubt first century Jews drank such fine spirits." I chuckled.

"True. One of the advantages of modernity. In any case, I want you to know that should you need my assistance, don't hesitate in the least to ring me up. I might also suggest you touch base with your predecessor, Father Watson. He's at an assisted living facility in Winona where he served earlier in his career."

I'd always preferred to start a new post with no preconceived notions, so I simply said, "Please send me his contact information."

"I'll e-mail it to you directly. I assume St. Aidan's e-mail hasn't changed."

"I assume it hasn't since e-mails keep rolling in, but if I don't hear from you there in a few days I'll get back to you." I jotted a note on the desk calendar three days hence.

"Very good, then," said Bishop Farley. "And Angus, you know God has led you here. I know you will be a good shepherd to your little flock on the island and also in Texas. He will guide you through any difficulties you might experience."

I thought of Millie, Thelma, Tom, and Penny. "Yes, Bob. Our God is faithful."

Bishop Farley ended the call, leaving me to wonder what other difficulties might await me.

Chapter 21

Bishop Farley, true to his word, had already sent Father Watson's contact information shortly after we'd ended his call. I then listened to and deleted several spam phone messages. I no sooner put the handset back in its receptacle when I immediately heard a series of cacophonous, discordant sounds emanate from the nave of the church.

"What in the world …?" I pushed myself off the luxurious chair and headed for the sanctuary where Thelma, seated at the organ, pressed on each of the three keyboards in turn with her left forearm. I waited for her to stop whatever she was doing, hopefully not practicing the postlude for next Sunday.

"Good morning, Thelma!" I announced as loudly as I thought necessary.

"Why, good morning, Father. What brings you to St. Aidan's today?"

The obvious answer was because I was the priest here and this was my calling and duty, but instead I said, "Why were you pressing on the keys with your arm?"

"Did you say there was a fire alarm? Oh, dear, we better leave immediately." She grabbed her briefcase and started to vacate the bench, but I stood in her way and shouted, "No, Thelma. Your arm!" I imitated her process on the nearest keyboard as she settled back into place.

"O, my arm composition. That's what you're wondering about?" I nodded my head repeatedly hoping she'd be able to translate my intentions. "One must occasionally clear out the pipes," she said. "Remove dust and ladybugs and evil spirits."

I opened my mouth and tipped my head back showing I understood. Dust and bugs, yes, but evil spirits? I really should not have been surprised. Episcopal churches have a history of attracting all sorts of folk including aging hippies, new-agers, spiritualists, and others a bit outside traditional Christianity. We are nothing if not inclusive.

"Well, I'll leave you to your process," I bellowed. "See you Sunday morning."

"Yes, Father. The next time I clear the pipes I'll give you fair warning."

Thelma wiggled on the bench, pushed a button under the middle keyboard, and launched into a ponderous, deafening rendition of "There'll Be Peace in the Valley for Me."

I walked away thinking that some music was better than nae music.

+ + +

I no sooner seated myself back at my desk when a virtual giant of a man in a brown and khaki uniform and Smoky Bear hat appeared at my office door.

"Good morning," I stood and said, somewhat taken aback by this obvious officer of the law.

"Sherriff Dave Messerli," the man said, offering a hand as large as a catcher's mitt. I came around my desk and reached for the shake, his hand wrapping around mine like a parent's around an infant's.

"Angus MacManus," I said, tilting my head back in an attempt to meet his eyes. "What can I do for you, officer?" I wondered if there had been complaints from the townsfolk regarding our piper or organist.

"I'm just here to introduce myself and to let you know I'm here to serve and protect." The look on his face was friendly, yet professional as our hands disengaged. "The calls from the island have been few, the last one regarding the annual decoration of your church by Bluestone High's graduating seniors."

"Ah, yes" I said, sure that Millie made that call.

He simply smiled at me and said, "Dennis O'Neill tells me you've installed some security cameras."

"Actually, Dennis installed them," I said, showing him the program on my computer that captures any movement, including his arrival at the church door.

"I think that should be sufficient to pick up any trespassers, probably animals mostly," he said, watching himself entering the church door. "Just so you know, in previous summers we've had calls regarding a threatening groundhog."

"Good to know," I said, chuckling.

Officer Messerli said, "I'm sure you know the 9-1-1 system. Most of the islanders have, shall we say, been around awhile. Falls, broken hips, and the like are not unexpected. Please call if you need anything."

I walked him out to his patrol boat with "Bluestone Police" painted on both sides of the hull, glad to know help was available, even protection from rogue rodents.

Chapter 22

Since Malcolm and Fiona provided breakfast on Mondays and Wednesdays, and Friday night was always fish, we were only responsible for simple breakfasts, lunches, and scattered dinners, as well as weekend meals. On Saturdays we imposed on Shorty to take us into town where we walked to our van parked at Fischer Ford and toured the neighboring communities, stopping for supper (dinner out east is called supper here) wherever we could find a cafe or a finer dining establishment. This made up for our Tuesday night meals, which I prepared and Mae tolerated. Her grocery list always included lots of fruits and vegetables, and occasionally to appease me, hot dogs and Hostess Twinkies.

At 2:00 every Thursday afternoon, Shorty's pontoon, laden with bags and boxes of groceries labeled with their owners' names, landed at the island dock. This became a sort of community happening where the whole island came together to collect their food and help those who needed help toting victuals to their cabins. It made my heart swell.

Until Millie's voice screeched, "What do you think you're doing?"

Millie had one grocery bag under her arm while the other hand clutched the edge of another Penny Burns had in her grip.

"You need help I'm just helping you carry your groceries to your cabin ..."

"I most certainly do not need help, especially from you. Now let go of that bag!"

Penny shook her head and let go of the brown paper sack as Millie clutched it and trudged off to her cabin.

"I only wanted to help," Penny said to whoever would listen.

Mae and I carried two bags of groceries each filled with our normal order plus the extras for the pot-luck cook-out tomorrow evening. Once out of earshot, Mae muttered, "Penny needs to back off before someone smacks her."

I couldn't help thinking that Millie could also use an attitude adjustment. I needed to find out what in her past she's hiding.

Chapter 23

The first Friday Fish Fry of June was cancelled because Malcolm and Fiona were absent, attending a planning event for the annual Scottish Fair and Highland Games held every year in Eagan, Minnesota, just south of St. Paul.

I'd found a gas barbecue grill in the storage shed behind our cabin, so had advertised the Sunday before that Mae and I would be hosting an island pot-luck. I would grill burgers and hot dogs; the other islanders and whatever townsfolk wished to attend would bring a dish to share and their own drinks.

I had no idea how this would go over, but was pleasantly surprised to have responses by Tuesday noon from 20 people, almost equally divided between islanders and townsfolk. Mae had e-mailed our grocery list, including burgers, hot dogs, buns, some soda – which Minnesotans call 'pop' – ketchup, and mustard to the Pick-Em-Up for Thursday delivery. I would have liked to add beer to that list, but didn't want to push Millie over the edge.

"I'm looking forward to this," I said to Mae. "I hope I haven't put you to too much trouble."

"I'm just thankful you discussed it with me before you announced it," she said, putting potluck necessities in a wicker basket.

"I've learned a few things over the year," I said. "You do not like surprises among them."

"True," said Mae. "Actually, I'm looking forward to a nice picnic on the grounds. People are always more talkative outside the church walls. More themselves."

"Indeed. It's hard to minister to people who have fences around their character," I said.

"You've always been good at keeping private matters private, except the rare ones you share with me, knowing I would never ever divulge a parishioner's problems to anyone," said Mae.

I put my arm around her shoulder and said, "And for that I am truly thankful. Without your ear I would have imploded long ago."

+ + +

Minnesotans obviously had made an art out of the potluck. I've never seen so many casseroles – which they called "hot dish," in my life. Fried chicken, cold pasta salads, and Jell-Os of various flavors and iterations – some topped with whipped cream and bananas, some infused with fruits or even vegetables – covered the tables Mae and I had appropriated from the church fellowship hall and covered with cheap colorful tablecloths we'd bought at an "Everything's-a-Dollar" store in St. Cloud.

The normally introverted Minnesotans seemed to change spots in the warmth of the summer sun and communal love of food. I never once had to prime the conversational pump or even bring a wallflower into the ruckus of talking and feasting. Even Harry Burns seemed to be enjoying himself, eating a burger and sipping from a can of Schell's while Penny was in her glory, gabbing to all. I noticed that Millie had simply stopped by, left a bag of potato chips on one of the tables, scowled, and left.

The evening wound down, many people practicing what we've learned was the "Minnesota good-bye" that could take up to twenty minutes. When the only revelers left were Mae, me, and Penny – who insisted on staying back to help us clean up – I was bone-tired, but happy the evening had gone so well.

"Mrs. MacManus you clean up the tables and Father and I will take them back to church you don't want those cheap tablecloths just throw them in the trash ...

Harry Burns had left long ago, leaving his wife to her customary schmoozing. I stood between Mae and Penny, saying, "We appreciate your kind offer to help, but please allow Mae and me to follow our custom of completing what we've begun. It will give us a chance to absorb the evening together." Actually, all I wanted was to avoid listening to Penny any more than I'd already heard that night.

"Oh well then I'll be on my way Harry is probably waiting for me anyway but are you sure you won't need help ...

"We'll be fine," I interrupted. "If we need help, you'll be the first one we'll call."

Penny kept at her version of the Minnesota good-bye until darkness fell. Once she had finally left, Mae said, "I'll pack up the leftovers; you fold up the tablecloths which I will wash and save for another use; we'll take the tables back in the morning. No rain on the horizon or on my phone's weather app."

What did I ever do to deserve such a wise wife, and when would I ever realize the greatness of God's grace?

Chapter 24

During Thelma's introduction to the processional hymn listed as #501, "O Holy Spirit, by Whose Breath," the sound of pages flipping like a flapping flock of pelicans filled the nave. Everyone knew Thelma was not only deaf, but also somewhat dyslexic, so the hymn that spring morning turned out not to be #501, but #105, "God Rest You Merry, Gentlemen," not at all liturgically correct, but still sung "lustily and with good courage" as John Wesley instructed.

A handful of folks from town who had not yet worshipped at St. Aidan's, however, were left scratching their heads wondering why the faithful at St. Aidan's were singing a Christmas hymn in June. The congregation had also learned to fulfill the law of Christ by bearing Thelma's burdens.

Ingrid Larssen sang a lovely setting of "Bread of the World in Mercy Broken" during the distribution of the sacrament, accompanying herself on the transept piano opposite the organ. I wondered if perhaps she could be persuaded to take a Sunday at the organ, but decided not to broach the subject with Thelma. One must, after all, pick one's battles.

When the last bombastic notes of Thelma's postlude ended, Penny hustled over and interrupted the conversation John Smyth had begun with Ingrid.

"You have the voice of an angel! I've never ever ever ever heard anything like it where did you get your training or maybe you were just born with it some people are born with it you probably were born with it and could sing like a canary since the age of one …"

Ingrid just smiled and glanced at John, hoping maybe he could extricate her from this embarrassing situation.

"Penny, if you don't mind, I'd like to escort Belle and Ingrid to coffee hour." With Belle on one arm, he offered Ingrid the other and led them away from Penny to the fellowship hall.

Penny shouted after them over the sound of the rest of the recessing congregation. "You have such a gift that beautiful voice belongs on a CD somewhere have you made a CD I'd love to have one just tell me where I can get it ...

Harry Burns, who had been sitting in the back pew that morning, appeared and followed his wife towards the fellowship hall, but turned left instead of right at the end of the hallway, walking out into the clear spring day.

Chapter 25

Penny, as usual, flitted about the second Wednesday morning breakfast in June, serving as an unnecessary waitress. In the best Minnesota style, everyone was more than capable of getting up and serving themselves from the warmers lining the wall by the kitchen and the beverage cart Penny had set in her usual manner, each glass and cup filled to exactly the same level and lined up like so many soldiers in review.

She carried a coffee carafe to Tom Cooper, bent over, and warbled lightly in his ear, "Would you like more coffee?" smiling and batting her eyes.

"No, thanks, Penny. I'm fine," said Tom, who was sitting at a table with John and Belle Smyth, Dennis and Trudy O'Neill, Mae, and me.

"You just let me know whatever you want I'll get it for you just raise your hand and wiggle your fingers and I'll be there, you folks, too," holding the coffee at the ready, nodding to the rest of us, then turning and calling to the kitchen, "Fiona! Fiona! This table needs more hash browns," before scurrying off to the next table. Fiona, dressed in a white chef's coat and hat, scowled at Penny through the kitchen's open bay.

Fiona walked over to check on our hash brown situation, scowled and said, "One of these days I'm going to cool her jets." We all told her we were fine hash brown-wise, so she went back to the kitchen and carried a tray of leftover cream puffs to the walk-in freezer.

"That Penny sure is a friendly one," said Trudy, to which Dennis nearly spit out his coffee.

"Friendly?" he said under his breath, recovering and swallowing. "I'd say more like oppressive." Belle Smyth just smiled and dabbed the corners of her mouth with a cloth napkin the Episcopal Church Women had embroidered many years ago in green with *St. Aidan's* on the corner.

I pushed my chair back and said, "Well, the pew bulletin won't write itself. If you'll excuse me ...." I stood, picked up my plate, cup, and silverware, carrying them to the kitchen, even though had I left them on the table Penny would certainly have taken care of it in her hyperactively helpful way.

The Macalesters sat on stools at the butcher block island, leaning on their forearms waiting for the breakfast crowd to finish. I poked my head through the bay window and said, "So, are the shoemaker's children without shoes this morning?"

"We'll eat once the rush is over," said Malcolm.

"And we can get some peace," said Fiona, sipping coffee, watching Penny clear tables.

"Well, thank you for another delightful repast. We all look forward to another Friday fish fry."

"Accompanied by chips with malt vinegar this week," said Malcolm. What Canadians call chips, Americans call French fries, even though they are not French at all, but originated in Belgium. Most people in the states prefer their chips – and some even eggs! – with ketchup. Barbarians!

How did this country ever survive its independence?

+ + +

After our Wednesday evening meal – egg salad sandwiches on wheat bread with lettuce, lightly-salted potato chips, and dill pickles – Mae and I set out for our weekly walk. The weather report called for cloudy skies with a chance of rain around 9:00, so we felt safe, intending to be back by 8:30.

Even considering the cast of characters both normal and odd at St. Aidan's, I was feeling more and more comfortable here. Priests, like everyone, are not one-dimensional, at least priests who keep their heads on straight. Ministry can become all-consuming, but in

94

my experience clergy who have interests outside the confines of their profession are more likely to thrive. Maybe that was my problem in Bicker Harbour. All work and no play made Angus a dull priest.

Hence poetry. Even bad poetry kept me sane, my latest effort being a limerick, which I recited to Mae on our walk:

A peaceful and tranquil isle
Certainly suits my lifestyle.
This wonderous place
With its quietous pace
Shall make me abide here awhile.

"Is 'quietous' even a word?" said Mae

"Of course it is. It's a neologism. I made it up. It means ..."

"I get it," interrupted Mae, holding her right hand in the air for emphasis. "I'm certainly glad our daily bread doesn't depend on your literary endeavors."

So I'm not J. K. Rowling or James Patterson, but they're not Angus Ian MacManus, are they?

Chapter 26

I peered at my laptop on Thursday morning, unsuccessfully willing the word processing program to outline my sermon, when Tom Cooper appeared at my open door. It has always been my custom to leave my office doors unlocked and open to welcome the stranger, as the Holy Scripture instructs.

"Father, might I have a word?" As always, he was the picture of an elegant gentleman, dressed in khakis pressed to a razor's edge and a green golf shirt with a little kangaroo on the pocket.

"Certainly, Tom. Please come in." He stepped in and quietly closed the door.

I stood and said, "Please have a seat," motioning to one of the two chairs in front of my desk. I walked around my desk and sat in the other chair, leaning forward to give Tom my full attention. He sat and kept both feet on the floor, then swallowed and somewhat nervously began.

"I have a situation with one of the islanders." He said no more, just looked at me and then at his feet. I waited.

"I don't know if you saw Penny talking to me by the oak tree last Monday." He said *talking* as if it were a double entendre.

"Sorry, I didn't."

"That incident was far from the first. It's just that ... well, it's been two years, but I'm still mourning Jennifer's passing, and I'm not looking for another relationship, *especially* not with a married woman."

"And you feel Penny is pursuing you?"

"Yes ... no ... I don't know. She's always so . . . helpful." Again, he said *helpful* as if it had a deeper meaning.

"Penny is definitely that," I said. "Have you spoken to her about this predicament in which you find yourself?"

"I'm not sure I can. I don't want to hurt her feelings, but whenever our paths cross, which happens often on the island, I feel so uncomfortable my tongue refuses to cooperate. And from my observation, I wonder about her relationship with Harry. He seems to avoid her as much as he can."

"Harry does enjoy fishing." I've also noticed Harry's attitude regarding Penny, but I refuse to insert myself into the condition of their marriage unless they came to me for counsel.

"So," said Tom, "what do you advise?"

I lifted my hands off my lap, folded them, closed my eyes, bowed my head, and leaned forward. I wasn't necessarily praying, but I should have been. Then I said, "I advise you to pray the Holy Spirit will give you the words you'll need at the right time. Then be alert for that time."

Tom inhaled deeply, exhaled, then stood like a man heading to the guillotine. I stood and waited.

"Thank you, Father. I guess time will tell."

"As it most often does," I said.

+ + +

As he approached the Burns's cabin, Tom heard Harry and Penny talking behind the closed door. He was not an eavesdropper, but maybe this was part of Father's advice about "the right time."

He was not about to knock on the door and confront them, but he couldn't help but hear Harry's raised voice and Penny speaking softly, apparently in an effort to calm her husband. Tom couldn't make out any words, just their argumentative mood.

Tom kept walking slowly past Harry and Penny's cabin, then heard a door slam. He turned his head slightly and glimpsed Harry Burns stalk to his dock, quickly unmoor his boat, start his inboard motor, and take off in an angry spray of lake water.

Tom, about twenty yards down the path, turned to his right, and out of the corner of his eye saw Penny standing at her cabin's door, arms wrapped around her middle. In the quiet of the late spring morning, he heard her snuffle and caught a brief glance as she wiped her eyes with the back of her hand, then stare at Tom for a moment before turning, gently opening her cabin door and going back inside, the silence of Penny's home contrasting with the roar of Harry's boat.

Chapter 27

Mae had become enthralled by a children's book written and illustrated by Warren Hanson about a woman who knits hats and gives them away. Mae had then taken on as her ministry knitting soft beanie caps for infants and children, then delivering them to the hospital and schools in Bluestone. Whether they were used or not was beside the point. It made her feel good, a way to love her neighbor as herself as Jesus taught, whether that love was returned or not.

"Mae, I have a proposition," I said, sipping coffee after Friday's breakfast of toaster waffles. A former parishioner had given me this particular mug in 2020 in the midst of the COVID-19 contagion. The whimsical text on the cup said "Priests like you are harder to find than toilet paper in a pandemic."

Mae sat on the love seat, her legs stretched out at a right angle to her torso, taking up the whole couch as she knitted another tiny multi-colored cap. She tipped her head back and looked at me over her reading/knitting glasses. My propositions, like rearranging the furniture, for example, were always met with a great amount of skepticism and always rejected.

I walked over to her, coffee in hand, and said, "As you know, St. Aidan's has installed security cameras."

"Mmm-hmm."

"And, well, I've been given the job of looking at whatever they capture, which so far has been basically nothing."

"Mmm-hmm."

"And, well, I'm thinking of delegating that responsibility."

"Mmm-hmm."

Here goes nothing.

"Might you be willing to take it on? It should only take a few minutes of your time whenever I ask you to come to the office."

Silence. Continued knitting.

"Well?"

"Shouldn't you be asking someone on the vestry to do it?" she said, still knitting, still knitting. I almost expected her to say 'Nevermore,' echoing Edgar Allan Poe's raven.

"That's the problem. Some of the visuals the cameras capture show other church members, and as their priest, I think it unwise for one parishioner to be ... spying, shall I say, on another." I knew this was a lame argument, but still.

Still knitting.

Finally, Mae stopped, sat up, laid her project and reading/knitting glasses on the couch, looked at me, and said, "But you think it's perfectly proper for your wife to do it."

"You're the logical choice," I said. "I feel highly uncomfortable doing it, and equally uncomfortable asking anyone else to do it."

She stood, walked to the kitchen sink, drew a glass of water, drank, then put the glass on the counter. She was making me sweat before she lowered the rejection boom.

She put her hands on the edge of the sink, leaned forward, looked out the window, and said, "No. Absolutely not. I will not be your partner-in-espionage."

Oh, well. Just another thing seminary didn't bother to teach us.

Chapter 28

The next Tuesday I did not limit my visits to those who worshipped at St. Aidan's, but finally stopped in at some of the other cabins on the island, which I should have done long ago. Some were happy to see me and tolerated my visits, others treated me like a Mormon missionary or Jehovah's Witness, not that I had anything against those branches of, but I knew the drill. When people saw men in white shirts and ties come up the walk, they turned off the lights and didn't answer the door. This is why I never wore a white shirt on the island.

Thelma was in her usual morning position, on hands and knees pulling Creeping Charlie out of her Moss Roses. I stood in front of her, bent over to her eye level, and said, "Good morning, Thelma. What beautiful flowers."

She startled for a moment, then straightened, looked at me, smiled, and said, "Yes, Father. We could use some showers, but it seems the weeds like rain more than my perennials."

I was getting a cramp in my left calf, so I stood and flexed my ankle. Thelma hopped up as well, repudiating what I believed old age to be like.

"I appreciated your postlude on Sunday," I said. "Was it Bach?" realizing Bach would have been appalled at her rendition.

She grew serious and said, "I would never play any of that rock music in church."

"No, of course not," I said, raising my voice and hoping she would understand.

"The closest I would ever get to rock music would be Brahms' Lullaby. My babies loved to be rocked. Stanley had the croup and could not fall asleep unless I rocked him, sometimes for over an hour."

"So, you were married?" She was not an old maid after all.

"I don't want to be buried. Cremate me and send me to the four winds."

+ + +

John Smyth sat on his porch swing reading the *Bluestone Gazette*. He wore a tie-dyed T-shirt, tan cargo shorts, and leather moccasins with no socks. I felt overdressed in white ankle socks, Dockers boat shoes, black slacks, and today, a blue short-sleeved clergy shirt with collar. One must dress the part from time to time, less people forget your office.

"Father, come and sit a spell," said John, seeing me at the foot of his walk and motioning me to the seat next to him.

"Thanks. I will," I said climbing the stairs to his porch and sitting next to the retired physician who folded his newspaper and put it on his lap.

"Another beautiful day on Bluestone," he said.

"That it is," I said. "Where is your good wife this morning?" They were seldom seen apart.

"She's inside plying her trade."

"Oh? Does she have a job?"

"Not a job, more of a useful hobby," said John. "She's knitting a baby blanket for the advent of our next grandchild due in September."

Serendipity?

"My wife knits hats for newborns," I said. "We'll have to get these two needle wielders together."

"Belle would like that. Before my retirement and our move to the island, she was quite active in a sewing group in town. Now we stick close to the island, worship here, and get away to see the grandkids when we can."

"How many grandchildren do you have?"

"Twenty-four with two more on the way. We're good Catholics."

"The Lord does preserve and extend His church," I said. "And where do your children live?"

"On the continent, San Jose to Boston and points in between. Beyond, the farthest is New Zealand. Anne was born with wanderlust. She's an obstetric nurse practitioner."

"Taking after her father." I changed the subject. "As a good Catholic, how do you view the worship at St. Aidan's?" I asked.

"Well, as you know, the Episcopal Church is known by us Roman Catholics as 'Catholic lite'."

"Ah, yes. The phrase coined by the comedian Robin Williams. Theologians have struggled to defend the church of Rome against something I doubt was ever intended."

"It all comes down do grace, doesn't it?" said John.

"Indeed it does," I said, "whether our poor efforts stem from Rome or Canterbury."

"And God preserve us all from our petty squabbles."

"I agree. Perhaps St. Aidan's, as a small slice of ecumenicalism, can play a part in healing the rift."

"Well, Father, I admire your lofty goal, but you only have us for six months at a time. Don't go getting any grand ideas."

"Believe me, I won't," I said, but then again, Jesus started with only twelve, and look where that got us.

Chapter 29

The third Thursday in June went as Mae envisioned. She'd planned a shopping trip, which meant I took the day off of my usual Thursday sermon planning and we were carried across the bounding main by Shorty Dvorak.

Mae shopped until I dropped, but not before we had a repulsive lunch at one of St. Cloud's three malls' food courts. By the time Shorty delivered us back to the island that evening, all I could do was drop to the mattress while Mae unfolded her purchase and hung them in the closet. What is it about shopping that gives women a surge of adrenalin?

I uncharacteristically slept until almost 8:00 Friday morning. Mae had the radio on in the kitchen to NPR world news. I rolled my legs out of bed, rubbed my face and thinning hair, showered, shaved, and dressed in another summer modified priest costume: khakis (I could not ever bring myself to wear short pants), and a bright green clergy shirt again with clergy collar. The shirt and collar reminded others – and me – of who I was.

Mae was standing at the kitchen sink, her hands submerged in soapy water. I crept up behind her, wrapped my arms around her midsection, kissed her left ear, and said, "Good morning, you."

"Don't get any ideas," she said. "We've got work to do."

"We?" That pronoun did not often bode well.

"Yes, we. Thanks to me, you missed your sermon prep day, so you need to work on that. Since this position did not come with a maid, I will be cleaning and washing clothes and doing other various household chores before the fish fry tonight. There's coffee in the pot and cereal in the cupboard." She lifted a plate out of the dishwater, rinsed it, and slid it into the drying rack. Old school, but satisfying.

Fish was not her favorite, but she was a good soldier and didn't complain. I didn't complain about the cereal, either, so we were even.

As soon as I stepped out of the cabin, I could tell sermon preparation would not come easy because a poem by James Russell Lowell intervened:

> *And what is so rare as a day in June?*
> *Then, if ever, come perfect days;*
> *Then Heaven tries earth if it be in tune,*
> *And over it softly her warm ear lays ...*

Yes, this was a day of days, not meant to be squandered in an office bent over a computer. I'd given enough sermons to know that, if necessary, I could wing it. Read the text, explain anything that needed explanation, apply the law so the congregation would rid themselves of any self-aggrandizement, then hit them with the Gospel that, though they were worms in the eyes of God, He loved them anyway.

Two well-used phrases came to mind: "Age and treachery defeat youth and skill" and "So it shall be written; so it shall be done." At least the last phrase had a theological connection, having been said by Yul Brynner in the 1956 movie *The Ten Commandments.*

So instead of my office, I sat on our dock, eyes closed, soaking in the sun and shimmering air while my brain worked on the homily.

No computer needed.

+ + +

By now the diners at the Friday Fries and Monday and Wednesday breakfasts had heard the prayer often enough. Some even were brave enough to say the Selkirk Grace with me this Friday eve:

105

Some hae meat and canna eat,
And some wad eat that want it,
But we hae meat and we can eat,
And sae the Lord be thankit.

The whole crowd responded with a loud "Amen."

"Before we get our food," I said in my best preacher voice, "we need to thank not only the Lord for the food, but also for Harry Burns and his fishing prowess. Harry, please stand and accept our gratitude."

All turned to the back of the hall where Harry sat alone, as usual. He scowled under his thick red beard, but half-stood to receive the applause from those gathered, then sagged onto his chair and tried to reclaim his inconspicuous position.

I never recalled anyone ever approaching Harry to even say a quick greeting. I guess they figured he was not the social kind since he always sat as far away from the crowd as possible. Some people are like that, introverts who prefer observation to conversation. Considering Harry's earlier visit with me, I didn't think this was the case. Something else was bothering him.

The line formed, loading plates with deep fried perch (my favorite), broiled walleye, fries, cole slaw with Fiona's secret dressing, and tonight, bread pudding for dessert with raisins and a touch of rum.

By act of the vestry, alcoholic beverages – except for the rum in the pudding – were banned from the Friday evening feasts due to an unfortunate incident several years ago involving two plastered townsmen and an argument about which was the better fishing lure, the Mepps spinner or the Lindy Rig.

As always, coffee, milk, and water were the offered, perfectly arranged on the beverage cart by Penny in her OCD way.

"Decaf or regular Mr. O'Neill you probably want regular since you are such a busy man but maybe you want decaf tonight … "

Penny was back to her old self, helping any and all who needed or didn't need her help. She stationed herself at the end of the line, chatting up everyone as they picked up their drinks from her well-organized cart.

"Well hello Thelma would you like some coffee?" Penny spoke slowly to our hard-of-hearing organist.

"Heavenly days, of course not." Said Thelma. "Toffee gets caught in my dentures." She picked up a glass of water, turned and spotted Belle Smyth at their usual table, then smiled and paraded to Belle's table like a teenager headed for her best friend.

Mae leaned to me over the serving line and mumbled, "She may be deaf, but she's not creaky." We should all hope to have Thelma's vitality when we reach her age, if we ever do.

"Leave me be! I'm perfectly capable of carrying a plate and a glass. I don't need any help, especially from you."

Millie TerHorst didn't care who heard her outburst. A hush fell over the crowd as Millie turned her back on Penny and marched to her customary spot next to Thelma Wadewitz. Thankfully, conversation soon returned to a normal level.

Mae and I each snatched a glass of milk from Penny, smiling but not conversing, then found seats with Tom Cooper and Maggie Claus, a secretary at a law firm in town and a regular attendee at mass.

Out of the corner of my eye I saw Fiona shake a spatula in Penny's direction. The ever-helpful Mrs. Burns leaned across the serving window talking to Malcolm. I excused myself and returned to the serving line intending to claim another perch and defuse the situation.

"Fiona and Malcolm, you've outdone yourselves again," I said, standing next to Penny. "The fish and coleslaw are absolutely delicious. I've never had better."

"Thanks, Father," said Malcolm, standing behind his wife, understanding my presence and its purpose. He looked from me to

Penny, who looked like innocence personified. "Like many things in life, timing is the secret. Too little time in the oil and the perch is undercooked; too much time and it's spoiled."

Penny smiled at Malcolm as Fiona scowled. "I'll just go back to the beverage cart people will want refills the coffee urn was almost empty ..."

As Penny kept talking and turned to go, Fiona growled while Malcolm put his arm around her waist, whispered something to her, and led her back over to the prep area, where she picked up a cleaver and chopped a head of cabbage in two with one whack.

Mae and I finished our meal, returned our plates to the washing bay where Malcolm took them and put them in the industrial dishwasher, awaiting their cleansing baptism at the end of the evening. Penny appeared behind us, several dishes in hand. We stood aside as Malcolm, expressionless, took the plates from Penny.

I said, "Penny, thank you for your helpful spirit. We are blessed to have you here." I didn't say that maybe she should back off a little.

"Oh, Father, I appreciate you saying that I just try to do what should be done I just love the chance to be around people ..."

I listened for a few moments as Penny went on and on until Mae gave my arm a gentle tug, so I smiled, nodded, and left the hall, my good wife leading the way.

+ + +

We walked hand in hand back towards our cozy cabin. I thought about what had happened with Penny and Fiona, when Mae said, "Do you think Penny is pretty?"

Hmmm. "Why do you ask?"

"Don't you go answering a question with a question. You seem to initiate conversations with her regularly," said Mae.

I chuckled and said, "I initiate conversations with Millie also, and she's ... well ... let's say she was hiding behind the door when loveliness of face and spirit were handed out."

"Then why do you even bother talking to Millie?"

I thought for a time and said, "Maybe Millie needs it much more than most, aye?"

We kept walking when Mae said, "Do you think I'm as pretty as Penny?"

"Why this fixation on Penny?"

"Answer the question, Father MacManus."

"Have you not been listening for the last 25 years?" I turned her and gave her my best gap-toothed smile, then said, "Besides, Penny is way too skinny for me."

I should have kept the attempt at humor to myself. The bruise on my shoulder should heal in time.

Chapter 30

Surprisingly, Tom Cooper wasn't sitting on his porch the next Tuesday morning. I heard what sounded like the radio or TV inside, his cabin, so I knocked. He opened the inside door and we looked at each other through the screen door.

"Good morning, Tom. How goes the battle today?"

"Well, hello, Father!" said Penny Burns, walking up behind Tom and looking at me over his shoulder, a dish towel draped over her shoulder. "Nice to see you what brings you out today would you like a cup of coffee I just made a fresh pot would you like cream or sugar …"

The sounds I'd heard were obviously not the TV or radio. The look on Tom's face was ten percent chagrin, 90 percent terror. Otis ambled up behind Tom, tail wagging, tongue hanging out displaying his silly grin.

"And a good day to you, Penny." Tom's eyes pleaded with me to deliver him from this situation. "I, uh, came to talk to Tom about a matter of some importance …."

"Oh, don't mind me I'll just be in the kitchen …" Tom swallowed and kept up his puppy dog begging look.

"Actually, I was hoping Tom could come to my office where we could talk in confidence." This was a lie, but I could turn it into the truth.

"And I'll be gone the rest of the day," said Tom, turning to look at Penny, "so I need to lock the cabin." His look told me that wasn't entirely true either.

"Oh, oh, well then, I'll just be on my way always something to do you know, idle hands and all …" She kept talking while she took the dish towel back to the kitchen and hung it on the oven handle. I took a step back as Tom opened the screen door as Penny smiled and stepped gingerly past me. "See you soon Father probably at breakfast tomorrow ..." Her words faded as she walked backwards towards her cottage.

Tom held the door open and motioned me in, then closed and locked the door behind us, turned to me, and said, "Am I ever glad to see you."

+ + +

Tom led me to his table and motioned for me to sit. He sat across from me, arms on the table, hands folded.

"So, Penny," I said. "Quite the conversationalist."

"She's been showing up and just ... well ... taking over," said Tom, uncharacteristically not making eye contact with me.

"By 'taking over,' you mean ..."

"Doing the dishes, sweeping the floor, even cooking. All without my urging or permission." Tom lifted his hands to his forehead, emotionally exhausted.

"And this troubles you."

"Yes, it troubles me!" he whisper-shouted, running his right hand through his perfectly cut and styled graying-blond hair.

I decided to cut to the chase. "Has she been physically romantic towards you?"

"Not ... no ... well ... she has this habit of putting her hand on my arm or shoulder."

"And how do you feel about that?"

Tom put his arms on the table, folded his hands, looked at me, and said, "First, I'm not over Jennifer and may never be; second, she's a married woman; and third, she *won't stop talking*!"

"You're saying you're not attracted to her."

"That's the understatement of the century," he said, gathering himself, standing and walking to the kitchen sink, turning his back to me. "I don't know … I guess I've decided she's just Penny being Penny."

"That may be, but her attention still bothers you. Have you spoken to her about your feelings?"

"I'm too polite to interrupt her. Call it a character flaw, but that's how I was raised." He walked back to the table, sat, closed his eyes, and leaned back in his chair, stretching his legs, being careful not to invade my space.

I considered Tom's words, then said, "Do you like to fish?"

He opened his eyes, slowly sat up straight, and said, "I used to, but haven't gone this year. Why do you ask?"

"Maybe fishing is the way to approach your problem," I said, leaning forward in my chair. "As you know, Harry Burns is quite the fisherman. Maybe you could ask him to tag along sometime, offer to bring a six pack? Being out on the lake may bring an opportunity to talk to him about his wife."

"I … I don't know if that's a good idea."

"Maybe not," I said, "but it's an idea worth pondering."

Tom stared at Otis, lying in a patch of sunlight in front of Tom's sofa.

"I've taken enough of your time, Father," he said, standing in a sign that it was time for me to go. "I'll think about it."

Tom walked me to the door, unlocked it, showed me out, and locked it behind me. He might be gone for the rest of the day as he'd mentioned earlier, but I had the feeling he wouldn't be leaving his cabin, and wouldn't be planning a fishing trip with Harry Burns.

Chapter 31

The book of Hebrews is not light reading, especially on a Thursday morning only four days before Sunday mass. St. Paul, or whoever wrote it, did not append a commentary, so I had to rely on whatever books were in my library for enlightenment. *The Church History* by the 4th century Christian historian Eusebius, while invaluable, always tended to put me to sleep, but I soldiered on for an hour before changing my sermon text to the gospel reading for next Sunday.

I liked St. Mark. His favorite words were "then" and "immediately." Mark cut to the chase, and would undoubtedly be annoyed at the number of articles, books, and commentaries written to explain his words. I could almost see him shaking his head.

I called up the liturgical calendar for Sunday on the computer and read again the lessons for the day, concentrating on Mark's story of the man with an unclean spirit who interrupted Jesus in the synagogue in Capernaum. I could really make some comparisons to St. Aidan's, but thought better of including such in a sermon meant to edify the faithful. Sermons are not the place to make enemies. Now vestry meetings …

I thought of all the things I'd longed to say in meetings over the years. My tongue was permanently scarred from the bitings it withstood. Mae's ears, on the other hand, had borne the brunt of my exasperations on many a night after yet another knock-down drag-out battle pitting one division of the congregation against its opposite: hand-made or store-bought ornaments for the Christmas tree; hardwood flooring or carpet in the youth room; white or red poinsettias in December; should the tower bell be rung five minutes before the service or exactly at the start of mass. None of my seminary classes touched on any of these terribly important issues.

I noticed movement at my office door and saw Penny standing there with the mail. She looked like she was about to cry.

"Good morning, Penny. How much fan mail have you brought me today?"

Without a word or a smile, she stepped to my desk and put a rubber-banded stack of assorted paper on the corner. Her lips quivered when she glanced at me, then she turned and left.

"Penny! Wait!"

She did not wait, which left me wondering what was troubling her, since she was not acting like the Penny I knew. All was obviously not rainbows and lollipops at the Burns house.

+ + +

A knock on my open office door startled me awake a little before noon. Eusebius toppled off my lap and landed at my feet. My sleep-bleary eyes tried to focus on the visitor.

Harry Burns stood there staring at me looking like the most stoic Scot this side of the Atlantic.

I stood awkwardly, still half asleep, and managed to say, "Harry! Come in, come in!" I motioned to a chair. He took two tentative steps and lowered himself onto it when I stumbled around my desk and sat in the adjoining chair.

"How's the catch going?" I said, breaking the ice with something important to him.

He cleared his throat and said, "Some days better than others. Always enough, though."

"God provides," I said, smiling. "Isn't that generally true of everything in life?"

His eyes drifted to the wall behind me, checking out my diplomas and a plaque that said, *"To be born Scottish is to be born privileged, not with a silver spoon in your mouth but with pipes in your blood and poetry in your soul."*

He cleared his throat again and, obviously nervous, shifted his weight in the chair. His red hair, beard, and moustache, wide shoulders under a green plaid shirt might have been imposing, but his body language suggested anything but.

He cleared his throat and said, "It's about my ... Penny," he whispered, looking behind him at the open office door.

I got up, walked behind Harry, shut the door to give us privacy. Before I sat, I said, "Would you like coffee?" He shook his head, but I took my coffee cup and sat across from Harry, turned my torso towards him, crossed my legs nonchalantly, mug in both hands and said, "So ... Penny."

I looked at Harry, who looked at my gray running shoes, a misnomer if ever there was one since for me running was a thing of the past. I waited.

Harry's gaze went up to my knees and he said, "You may have noticed that she's ... well ... different."

"How do you mean?" I said, knowing full well what he meant.

Now he looked me in the eyes and said, "You mean to tell me you haven't seen how ... how ..." He twirled his hands, looking for a word. "Bossy isn't quite the right word ..."

"She's extremely helpful," I said. "Where did you meet Penny?" He sat quietly, as if in thought.

"We grew up together in Warroad, way up north."

"So, you've known her since childhood and the friendship blossomed into romance."

"You might say that ..."

I waited, but Harry just breathed heavily like he was nervous, so I took a sip of coffee and said, "Are you sure you don't want some coffee?" He shook his head and stared at my shoes again.

Then an idea. "It's almost after noon. Can I interest you in a beer?" Nothing like something liquid to lubricate the tongue. I'd be willing to give up a can of Cinnaster to help a parishioner.

He looked up at me then, the first eye contact of the meeting, and said, "Beer sounds good, but maybe another time."

He suddenly stood and said, "I'm sorry. I thought I was ready to talk about this, but I guess I'm not." Without another word, Harry Burns turned and lumbered out of my office.

It's not like I'd never encountered a troubled soul, but Harry's visit, especially after my conversation with Tom Cooper and his latest encounter with Penny, generated more questions. I'd have to wait until Harry was ready.

I'll also have to remember to keep extra Cinnaster handy.

Chapter 32

Millie greeted me with her characteristic bluntness the last Tuesday afternoon in June, glaring at me through her screen door, a cigarette dangling from her lip, graying black hair going every direction but right.

"What do you want? If it's lunch, I've already had it."

"Good day, Millie. May I come in?" This beanpole must subsist on one carrot a day and water.

"I suppose it would be unchristian of me to say no," she said, hesitantly opening her inside door and waiting for me to show myself in.

The first impression of my first real look at Millie TerHorst's abode was summed up in one word: austere. No pictures or paintings hung on her walls; all furniture was wooden, built by Amish craftsmen by the look of it; nothing that showed of comfort, solace, or consolation. In short, Millie's living quarters were a mirror of her. With a name like "TerHorst," she was undoubtedly raised a Puritan.

I wondered why two chairs flanked the kitchen table. I stood while Millie faced me from across the living space, "living" taken loosely.

I cleared my voice and said, "You'll be happy to know the security cameras are working well. I've seen parishioners coming to mass and a raccoon loitering around the church on Sunday evenings."

Millie stood as stiff as a flagpole and said, "Is there anything else?" Her stare was enough to scare a mosquito off a forearm.

"I, er, thought we might talk for a bit, get to know each other better."

"I live here," she said, "and you are the clergyman of, unfortunately, the only church on the island. I only agreed to be on the vestry because it needed a voice of reason and to make sure that tart Penny kept her nose out of church affairs. That's all you need to know about me and all I care to know about you."

She walked to the door, held it open, and my visit with Millie TerHorst ended.

+ + +

The first time I met Malcolm and Fiona Macalester – the next stop on my path – I'd learned, beside their culinary skills, that Fiona was fiercely proud of her Scottish heritage, so I took a chance on using my extremely rudimentary Gaelic.

I knocked on the frame of the open front door and announced loudly, "Feasgar math!" pronounced "fiskair mah," Scottish Gaelic for "Good afternoon" or "Good evening."

Fiona appeared, pushed the door open and me aside, then stepped outside, closed the door, and whispered, "Feasgar math," followed by twenty seconds of the mother tongue, the meaning of which I had no clue.

"I'm afraid you have me at a disadvantage, Fiona. My Gaelic is elementary, at best." She put a finger to her lips in the universal sign for quiet, then took my arm and led me down the steps toward the lake.

"My husband takes his rest every day at this time. I would not want to disturb him," she said, turning to look out over the blue water on this pleasant day.

"I understand," I said in a normal voice now that we were at a distance from the Macalester's cabin. "Nothing should come between a man and his nap. I'm just here on a friendly visit to see if there's anything I can do for you since you do so much for St. Aidan's."

Fiona kept her attention on the lake and said nothing. After enough time had elapsed to make me uncomfortable, I said, "Is there something you need to say, Fiona?" I was prepared for a tirade concerning Anglicanism.

"Perhaps God brought you here during Malcolm's time of respite for a reason," she said, finally turning to look at me. She said nothing. I waited. She opened her mouth, then closed it. I waited. "It's about that Penny Burns," she finally said. "Besides being a disgrace to the name, she … well … I trust Malcolm. Her I do not."

"I'm not sure I understand," I said, fully understanding.

"She may be totally innocent in her own eyes, but she's not in mine. Her constant flirting with Malcolm aggravates me. Malcolm just shrugs it off, but I cannot."

Thinking of the Scripture's instruction regarding interpersonal relations, I said, "Have you discussed your feelings with Penny?"

"No," said Fiona. "First of all, I fully doubt I'd get a word in, and second of all, I'm afraid I might do something drastic, no matter what she might say."

"What do you mean by 'drastic?'"

She looked back over the lake and said, "Let's just say she better hope I don't have a butcher knife in my hand the next time she tries to violate my space … or my husband's."

+ + +

I needed respite myself after those upsetting visits, so I headed to the church and the relative safety of my office. Dennis was fighting the good fight with the front door, still at work on the pneumatic opener.

"Hullo, Dennis," I called softly, not wanting to frighten him lest he fall off the small ladder. He held the new opener in his left hand, screwdriver in his shirt pocket, two long screws clamped between his lips. He turned his head slightly to acknowledge me, then stepped down and took the screws out of his mouth.

119

"I didn't mean to interrupt your work," I said. "Just wondering how things are going on the door front. Looks like you've got it under control." The parish could certainly afford a new door, but as aggravating as this project was, I could see Dennis enjoyed the challenge.

"You'd think so," he said, "but this door is a perennial problem. I really think the whole casement needs replacing. It won't hold a screw anymore no matter how I massage it." He frowned at the holes that were supposed to held the opener in place and shook his head.

"Say, while I have your ear, did you happen to borrow anything from the desk in the office when you were installing the security system?"

He furrowed his brow in thought and asked, "Not that I recall. Is something missing?"

"Just my monogrammed pen." I didn't mention the letter opener previous parish members gave me on my 40th birthday inscribed "From Norm and Connie."

"No, I wouldn't have had use for it." He patted his chest and pulled a fat rectangular carpenter's pencil out of his pocket. "After all these years, this is what I use when something needs writing. I've been kidded about it quite a bit over the years. Trudy has even threatened to buy me a subscription to the non-existent 'Writing-Instrument-of-the-Month' club."

I chuckled and said, "Well, a missing pen isn't a reason to call in the FBI. It's just that it's a well-loved and well-used gift from my wife."

"Oh, boy," said Dennis, rolling his eyes. "Whenever I lose something Trudy gave me, or even forget it was she who gave it to me 25 years ago, the dog house awaits." Then he looked up and said, "But now that you mention it, small things like spatulas, candles, or little bottles of oregano have gone missing over time. They're nothing expensive or irreplaceable, so the vestry never acts on it other than to hear complaints outside of our monthly meetings from Millie."

I nodded my head and said, "Well, if you come across a pen with my initials on it – AIM – please corral it for me."

"Will do," said Dennis. "Now if you don't mind, this door won't fix itself."

I nodded in agreement and said, "And sermons don't write themselves, either, much to my dismay, so you carry on with your ministry and I'll plow ahead with mine."

I stepped around Dennis's stool and headed for my office, wondering if perhaps St. Aidan's membership contained a kleptomaniac.

+ + +

I'd checked in with everyone on my list for today except Penny, and no way had I the energy to tackle that visit. She'll no doubt be at breakfast tomorrow morning. Call me a bad priest, but I've been making a mental note to be home with Mae most weeks at the normal time of the mail drop.

I leaned back in my lavish chair and closed my eyes to ponder the gospel for Sunday when I heard an almost inaudibly soft plop. I opened my eyes and saw Cranmer on the corner of my desk staring at me like he was the Great Sphinx of Giza.

"Hello, Cranmer. The Lord be with you." He did not respond with the customary "And also with you," but padded slowly and silently toward me, stopped behind my empty pen holder, brushed his chin on it once, then looked at me.

"Nice of you to notice my missing pen. Now can you tell me where it is?" Where is Doctor Dolittle when you need him?

Cranmer sat on his haunches looking at me like the superior beasts cats fancy themselves. Then he turned, hopped off my desk, reminiscent of Carl Sandburg's poem "Fog."

The fog comes
on little cat feet.

It sits looking
over harbor and city
on silent haunches
and then moves on.

Our cathedral cat padded languidly to my door where he stopped, sat, licked his left paw, stood on all fours, turned and stared at me for ten seconds, then left for parts unknown.

Chapter 33

"Breakfast awaits. Shall we?" I said, offering an arm to my wife.

"If we must, we must," she said. She would be supremely content staying put and dining on a stale bagel. She took my arm and we stepped out into what promised to be another one of those rare days in June, sun warm and humidity low.

We strolled arm-in-arm into the fellowship hall a little after 7:30. The room was buzzing with a full crowd, many of whom I'd never seen, undoubtedly townsfolk. We got in line behind John and Belle Smyth.

"How are the Smyths this fine day?" I said. John turned to me and said, "We are as fine as fuzz on a peach. And how are you two?"

Belle turned slowly and smiled at Mae, the two giving each other a light hug. Mae was nothing if not sensitive to the aging population. She could be testy with me at times, but especially with Belle, she was as soft as Cranmer's fur. The two had been knitting together and talking the talk of like-minded women on Tuesday afternoons.

"Quite the crowd this morning," I said to John. noting that every table was occupied.

"Word got out, undoubtedly by text, that along with honest-to-goodness real scrambled eggs, Malcolm and Fiona are serving biscuits and gravy today. Our chefs have been offered a substantial amount of money for their recipes without success," said John. "I hear Malcolm mixes cream with the eggs," John whispered.

I noted several diners tapping on their cell phones, surely letting friends and family in Bluestone and its environs know about the gourmet breakfast at St. Aidan's this morning. A flotilla of boats would soon arrive and tie off at the docks surrounding the island. As we waited in line, I noticed Penny and Harry Burns standing in the far corner of the hall, obviously arguing from Penny's body language. They weren't speaking loudly, obviously not wanting anyone to hear, but it was obvious to me that whatever they were discussing was troublesome. Then Penny's shoulders slumped, her chin dropped as she turned and hurried out of the fellowship hall, wiping her eyes on her sleeve. Harry followed, not stopping to engage anyone in conversation.

The Smyths were busy filling their plates, John helping Belle, so they didn't notice Penny and Harry. I looked at Mae, who lifted her eyebrows, sighed, picked up a plate, and began filling it with scrambled eggs. I followed suit, adding the biscuits and gravy and a scoop of melon for my daily requirement of fruit, lest Mae yet again put peas in the Jell-O.

+ + +

Mae prepared a light supper on Wednesday evening of a classic Waldorf Salad and breadsticks. After we did the dishes and put the leftovers in the refrigerator, we set out on our weekly Wednesday evening walk, donning light jackets against gray clouds and a cooling breeze. I grabbed an umbrella before we left the cabin just in case. We'd learned weather in the Midwest could be fickle.

Wednesday had become my "unofficial official" day off. The congregation knew of this since I listed it as such on the parish calendar, and graciously let me observe the midweek sabbath. So far nothing had happened to disturb it.

Since I was "off the clock," I was wearing my favorite yellow polo shirt under my gray windbreaker and the old tan chinos Mae threatened to replace on many occasions. Since they had become form-fitted to me over time, I'd successfully argued to keep them in my half of the closet. Like many a smart husband, I'd learned never to critique my wife's wardrobe.

Half way through our hand-in-hand island stroll, I stopped and turned to look at my wife. She gave me that look that meant, "Now what do you want?"

Since Jesus taught us to be persistent in prayer, I said, "Would you consider coming out of your retirement role of a woman-at-leisure?"

She squinted at me and said, "I'm happy being a 'woman-at-leisure,' as you say, catching up on my reading, knitting, and listening to Minnesota Public Radio."

I needed to step up my persuasive powers. "This won't take up any more of your time then is already being taken up accompanying me to meals at church. More of a friendly conversation kind of thing."

"And why can't you have this 'friendly conversation kind of thing'?" she asked, eyebrows raised.

"Well, I can and I do have friendly conversations, but there are certain things people will just not share with a priest," I said.

"And what makes you think they will share them with me?" I had to think fast, so I went for the obvious.

"Because you are a woman, and other women will often confide things to other women they would not confide to a man, especially with clergy." I could tell she was thinking from the way she looked away and her silence.

"And you want me to share with you what is revealed in these clandestine conversations?" she said.

"Well, yes. If you feel uncomfortable sharing any information you deem super-private, I would never press you."

She turned to look at the now gray, choppy waters of Bluestone Lake. Then she turned to me and said, "Let's get home before it starts to rain." The wind had just begun to pick up. No precipitation yet, but we could smell it coming. We headed for home just as Fiona's pipes began skirling from the other side of the island. Cabin lights flickered off, then back on a moment later.

It took five minutes for us to reach our cabin, just as raindrops big as old-time silver dollars splatted on the walk. We hustled inside and listened to the steady drumbeat of the storm assault the cabin's roof.

Blinking displays on our digital clocks indicated the power had indeed gone out and then came back on when we saw the island lights flicker.

"I hope Fiona found cover," said Mae, hanging her coat in the closet. "I'd hate to think of her, not to mention her pipes, soaked to the core."

"I have a feeling Fiona can handle a little rain," I said. "If she'd been at the Battle of Culloden in 1746, Scotland may well have won."

Mae knew I loved the history of the homeland and indulged me. She was much too practical to share my interest, even though she'd been a history teacher. I'd often teased her about not being a real Scot, even though her pedigree was equally as valid as mine.

The storm finally abated to a gentle drizzle, and I busied myself making a pot of decaf to ward off the chill that followed the storm. We used a percolator, the only way to make decent coffee, in my estimation. The only reason I chose decaf was the late hour, and my need for a good sleep before tackling Sunday's sermon in the morning.

I poured two mugs, handed one to Mae who sat in the loveseat paging through the Reader's Digest. I sat next to her, crossed my legs, took a sip, took a deep breath, and said, "By any chance, did you borrow my pen?" She knew exactly to what pen I was referring. No other pen would even be worthy of the question, but she asked anyway, "Are you referring to the Montblanc engraved with your initials?" Her tone of voice and evil squint told me trouble brewed.

"I'm sure it's in my office somewhere. You know I'm getting forgetful in my approaching frailty. It's probably in my chair cushion or used as a bookmark." I took another sip of coffee and tried to appear unconcerned, putting my arm around my wife, settling in for a nice snuggle, the rain playing a continuous gentle rhythm on the cabin roof.

After a few minutes of coffee sipping and one-armed snuggling, she said, "The answer is no."

I paused in mid-sip, lowered my mug, and said, "What was the question again?"

"You asked two: Did I borrow your pen, and would I have 'friendly conversations' with parishioners. The answer to both is 'no.'"

"Not even a yes to the first question if I find the Montblanc?"

"Not even," she said, glaring at me. "You do your thing and I'll do mine, which is being a woman of leisure." Then she half-smiled, put her coffee mug on the end table, and returned to the Digest. "And, by the way," she said, "Saturday you and I are hitching a ride with Shorty Dvorak to the mainland, hiking to our car, and spending another day shopping in St. Cloud. I need a place less surrounded by water. I'm beginning to feel like Noah's wife, whatever her name was."

"Naamah," I said.

"What?"

"Noah's wife's name was Naamah."

Mae looked at me sideways and said, "Whatever. Be sure to wear comfortable shoes."

I could find many more pleasurable and productive ways to spend a Saturday, but I gave my assent with silence, then sipped more coffee and thanked God for giving me a strong-willed wife.

Chapter 34

The shopping trip last Saturday went as I expected, Mae paging through racks and racks of clothing while I busied myself catnapping on chairs and benches.

We were relaxing the last Thursday evening in June after our supper of slightly-wilted leftover Waldorf salad. Around 8:00 Mae was reading and I was playing Wordle on my cell phone in an attempt to keep my brain engaged while I wasn't writing a sermon.

Suddenly Mae said, "What's that racket?"

"Sounds like a flock of crows," I said, hearing cawing from the trees behind the church.

"It's a murder," said Mae.

"You mean someone's been murdered and these crows know?"

Mae turned to me, tipped her head to look at me over her reading glasses, and said, "A group of crows is called a murder, not a flock."

"Ahh, yes. Thanks for reminding me," I lied.

My attention returned to the game on my phone when a dog, insistent and emphatic, barked and bayed at our door. I ignored it, thinking it must be Otis chasing a rabbit. Tom would move him along, but the racket continued. I hoisted myself off the couch and went to the door.

It was Otis, but he wasn't chasing anything. He stood looking at me, barking and whimpering alternately. He had put on some weight in his old age (but then, who hasn't?), jumped about two inches, did that pitiful whine dogs do, tried to twirl in the dog way of saying "Come with me right now! Timmy's in the well!"

"What is it, Otis?" I'd only been around the dog a time or two. He had been calm, even nearly comatose, if not friendly to me. I decided to play along. He turned and walked about three yards, then turned to make sure I was following. He led me to Tom Cooper's front door, where I heard Tom retching and moaning.

"Tom," I called through the screen door, "are you OK?" which was a patently foolish question since he obviously was not. I opened the door and saw Tom sitting on his couch, a plastic pail between his legs. He had obviously been vomiting, his face red, his shirt soaked in sweat. He breathed as if he'd just finished running a marathon. I took my cell from my pocket, pressed the home button and said, "Call John Smyth." When he answered, I told him of the emergency at Tom Cooper's cabin.

"Hold on, Tom. Help is on the way."

+ + +

"Tom, have you eaten anything? Taken any drugs?" said John Smyth, kneeling next to the obviously ill man.

He had all he could do to wave towards his table. John walked over and showed me what appeared to be small blue grapes.

"Huh. Looks like Moonseed," said John. "See if you can get some milk down him. Give me your cell. I'll call 9-1-1."

I went to Tom's refrigerator and found a quart of milk, then got a glass from his cupboard, filled it half full and tried to get him to take a sip while John explained the situation to the 9-1-1 operator.

He clicked off and said, "EMTs are on the way, Tom. Try to drink some milk, and don't be shy about puking."

+ + +

Once Tom was safely on his way to Bluestone Memorial, I asked John, "What did you call those grapes?"

John had picked up the remaining plants with a paper towel and put them in a Ziploc bag he found under Tom's sink and sent them along with the EMTs.

"Moonseed. They grow wild in the woods around here. Highly poisonous, like Oleander. Once or twice every summer some kid will mistake them for wild grapes and end up in the emergency room," he said. "I never took Tom for being the type to eat anything sketchy, though. I'll get a ride into town and check on him."

I went home to tell Mae what happened, then sank into the couch, put my head in my hands, and prayed.

+ + +

John knocked on our door right after sundown. After I let him in, he said, "Tom will be OK. They're pumping him full of fluids. He should be home tomorrow, weak but alive."

"Thank God," I said. "Did he say anything about why he was eating wild berries?"

"Yes. He said Penny brought them and he didn't have the heart to refuse. I'll have to have another talk with her."

Chapter 35

Mae and I were at the dock when Shorty Dvorak returned Tom to the island Friday morning. We walked with him to his cabin and went in to make sure he was settled. He thanked us, then apologized for not offering us anything to drink before plopping on his couch and saying, "I'm not a violent man, but Penny better watch out. I've had it with her."

I glanced at Mae and said, "Tom, if you need anything, you have my number. Don't be shy about calling."

"Thanks, Father. I will. For now, I just want to sit and stew awhile, drink water, and purge my system of the last of Penny's poison."

"I'm sure it was an honest mistake," I said, trying to put the best construction on the situation.

"A nearly fatal honest mistake," said Tom, his face uncharacteristically filled with anger.

+ + +

Writing a homily, while part of my calling and not always easy, tended to put me in a state of contemplation, so after making sure Tom was settled and as healthy as possible, I said farewell to him and Mae, then went to the church office to work on my homily for Sunday.

I'd been told at some point in time to never turn off a computer, so since I was not technologically advanced and not curious enough to know why, I followed that advice.

Then why was the MacBook powered off?

"Oh, well," I thought, turning the computer on, not giving the situation a second thought. Once the MacBook booted, I clicked on my sermon folder and then on the file for Sunday, July 3.

Why was the July 3 file blank?

I knew why. Because I am too old-fashioned and self-reliant. I recalled a pop-up window I ignored when I first started at St. Aidan's asking if I'd like the word-processing program to automatically save my files. I was certainly able to save my own files and didn't need a computer to do it for me, but when the power was interrupted by the storm on Wednesday, I'd lost what I'd written on Tuesday.

Well, live and learn. I started retyping what I could remember and kicked myself, promising to find the command to automatically save my work. Maybe.

+ + +

When Mae and I entered the fellowship hall that afternoon for the fish fry, I saw Harry and Penny again having an animated discussion in the back of the hall where Harry always sat, far from the crowd. Penny was gesturing wildly, stage whispering something I couldn't make out. Harry sat there, taking Penny's rant without response, then stood and left, avoiding me and anyone else who might want to greet him. His face looked like the most stoic Scot this side of Glasgow. He didn't hurry, just walked with purpose like the Marine he'd been, or still was since "once a Marine, always a Marine." When he reached the door, he stopped and leaned against the jamb for just a moment, then straightened and went on his way. Penny sat in Harry's vacated chair, stared at the door through which her husband had departed, then leaned forward as if in prayer before getting up and smiling her way to the beverage cart.

Chapter 36

Most clergy do not work on Saturdays, preferring to let their sermon preparation during the week incubate before the "show" on Sunday morning, but today, due to the situation with Tom Cooper and my stupidity with the computer, I needed to at least review the new outline of my homily, so I skipped breakfast with Mae and got to my office by 7:00.

I'd left the computer on when I left the office yesterday, didn't I? Then why was the computer off? Was it "sleeping"? No, it was definitely powered off because it didn't awaken when I pressed the space bar. Had another storm interrupted power on the island? No, that wasn't it.

"Huh. I'm definitely losing it," I thought. Then I noticed that no activity appeared on any of the camera feeds, which seemed odd, yesterday being Friday. But on to what I was here to do. I clicked on the sermons folder and opened the file for July 3.

Praise the Lord, the re-written sermon appeared. At least I hadn't lost it again. I finished reading the first two paragraphs when agitated footsteps pounded down the hall. I adjusted my trifocals as Harry Burns burst into my office.

"Have you seen Penny?" he said, out of breath.

"Is there something wrong?" I said, standing to look Harry in the throat, since he had at least a foot on me.

"Have you seen her?" he yelled, nearly frantic, his hands clenched.

"Not since last night at the Fry," I said.

He immediately turned and ran down the hall and out the door. I followed him and by the time I stepped out of the church, he pounded at Millie TerHorst's door.

"This will not end well," I thought, walking with as much speed as I could muster. Millie yelled something at Harry through her screen door before he spun and headed to the next cabin. Millie was half in and half out of her doorway, shouting at Harry's back.

"I wouldn't have anything to do with that woman! I hope you never find her!"

+ + +

Harry was off to the next cabin. Should I follow? I thought Penny probably stopped in to visit Tom Cooper. I was not about to catch up with Harry and kick over that hornet's nest, so I returned to my office and my sermon outline. Then I remembered what I did last night before the Fry and whacked myself in the forehead.

I recalled the great church reformer Martin Luther's quote: "Whoever drinks beer, he is quick to sleep; whoever sleeps long, does not sin; whoever does not sin, enters Heaven! Thus, let us drink beer!" Yes, beer is good, but frozen beer is not. I'd put a can in the freezer last evening before the fish fry, planning to liberate it after the meal, take it home, and enjoy it before bed, per Luther's excellent logic. But I'd completely forgotten about it.

I cursed myself as I went to the kitchen to dispose of the ruined ale and bemoan my forgetfulness. Cranmer met me there, sitting on the counter, meowing. "And good morning to you, Cranmer," I said. I'd been told he was self-sufficient, finding mice and other small creatures on the island for his subsistence and drinking lake water, but maybe he hadn't had much luck hunting lately. Maybe there were a few leftover morsels of fish in the locked freezer.

The key was not in its usual place above the freezer door. I remembered seeing a group of duplicates in my desk drawer, so I trudged back to my office, plucked a key attached to a small white cardboard circle labeled "Freezer," and headed back to the kitchen.

Still profaning myself for ruining a choice can of ale, I fumbled with the spare key as Cranmer hopped off the counter and glided silently over, rubbing against my right shin, then walking toward the deluxe oven/range opposite the freezer. I followed his path and saw the original freezer key on the floor.

"Whoever cleaned up last night after the fish fry must have dropped it here," I thought, picking it up and putting it back where it belonged. I inserted the spare key in the padlock, turned it right, pulled the lock down to hear the satisfying click of the now open lock, which I took off the freezer door and placed on the counter. Then I pulled the door open as the overly-bright LED lightbulb inside the freezer automatically came on.

I stepped back, let the freezer door close on its own, then took my cell phone out of my pocket and dialed 9-1-1.

Chapter 37

"9-1-1. What's your emergency?"

"This is Father MacManus at St. Aiden's on the island. I ... I ... I'm afraid one of my parishioners has had an accident."

"Is the person breathing?"

"I don't know ... I don't think so ..."

"Please stay on the line. I will notify the sheriff and get help on the way."

I put my phone on speaker and carried it with me to my office and called John Smyth on the church's line. Thank God I'd printed out my congregation's contacts and taped them to a corner of my desk.

"This is John. How may I help you?"

"John! Thank ... thank ... God you're there," I stammered. I was nearly out of breath from shock.

"Father? Is that you?"

"Yes ... John ... I need your help ... in the ... kitchen at church. Please hurry."

I hung up without getting an answer from John and carried my cell back to the kitchen. The 9-1-1 operator stayed in touch, assuring me help was on the way.

The sound of a powerful boat broke the morning stillness at the same time John Smyth arrived no more than 20 seconds after my call. He strode confidently to me and said, "What seems to be the problem, Father?"

I opened the freezer door and motioned John to look inside. He saw what I'd seen, and immediately stepped into the freezer, knelt next to the body lying on its right side, right hand grasping its left shoulder.

He lowered his head and shouted, "Can you hear me?" He used two fingers to check for a pulse, then looked up at me and said, "Have you called 9-1-1?"

"Yes ..."

"Then let's wait for the authorities to arrive."

I heard footsteps behind me and turned to see all six feet six and 300 pounds of Sheriff Dave Messerli. He saw John Smyth in the freezer and said, "What have we got, Doc?"

"Female. She has a pulse, but it's weak. Have the EMTs get her to the emergency room ASAP."

"They tied up at the dock right behind me. Father, please come with me. Doc will let the crew know what needs to be done."

Sheriff Messerli led me to my office. When we got there, I was too keyed up to sit. Sherriff Messerli stood, I paced.

"Tell me what happened," said Messerli.

"I came in early this morning to work on Sunday's sermon ... when I remembered I'd left a can of ale in the freezer last night after our fish fry ... frozen beer is spoiled beer, so I went to the kitchen to dispose of it before the can ruptured ..." I was talking so fast I had to sit from the effort.

"Sounds like you have some experience with frozen beer," said Sherriff Messerli, changing the subject in an attempt to calm me.

"Well, yes. My wife sometimes wonders if old age is catching up to me. The freezer was locked. There have been some issues in the past with interlopers in the church, so the vestry chose to institute several security issues, one of which was to keep the freezer locked, but the key wasn't in its usual place, so I went to my office to get the spare."

"Then what?"

"I opened the padlock with the spare key, then the door, and saw ..." I was too overcome to continue.

"And then?"

"I ... I wasn't sure what to do, so I called 9-1-1, then John Smyth. He got here just before you arrived. I've never experienced anything like this before." I dropped my head and stared at the floor, feeling like a fool.

The sheriff took a pen and a small notebook out of his pocket and jotted a few notes.

"How do you think she got locked in there? She obviously didn't do it herself."

"I don't know," I said, although several theories bounced in my brain.

"Do you know of anyone who might want to harm her?"

"She's a very helpful woman. Some people think she's too much so, but I can't comprehend that anyone would want to harm her," I said, while thinking of Millie's outburst, the look on Fiona's face last evening, and Tom's issues.

John Smyth appeared at my office door. "Dave, the EMTs are ready to transport. I'll ride along. Father, might you ask your good wife to go and keep Belle company? Let her know I'll be back as soon as I can."

I looked at Dave Messerli, who nodded his head. I ended my cell's connection with 9-1-1 and called Mae's cell to explain the situation.

"I'm on my way," said Mae. I took a deep breath, looked at Dave Messerli and said, "Sheriff, do you mind if I stay here for a time?"

"Please do. You've had quite the morning." He leaned against my desk, waiting for me to get my breath rate back to normal. Then he jotted in his notebook and said, "I'll be heading back to the mainland now," he said. "Once I check in at the hospital, I'll call and give you an update. In the meantime, if you think of anything that might be helpful, call." He took another card from his breast pocket, put it on the corner of my desk, and walked out.

As I tried to gather my thoughts, I looked at the laptop and it hit me like a sack of frozen perch.

"The security camera ..."

I tried to stabilize my brain, so I prayed for calm and wisdom. I needed to find Harry Burns and then call Dave Messerli.

Chapter 38

I exited the church's front door and saw Harry to my left plodding down the circular island path. He probably stopped at all the cabins on the island in what I now knew was a fruitless search for his wife. It was up to me to tell him the truth.

I stood in the middle of the walkway and waited for Harry to approach. He was still agitated, looking toward the cabins. He stopped in front of me and looked in my eyes. I stood my ground, let my bottom jaw drop, and took a deep breath but couldn't yet get my tongue to say what needed to be said. Birds chirped, oak leaves fluttered in the light breeze, sunlight shimmered on the lake.

I closed my mouth, swallowed, and said, "Harry, there's been an accident. Penny's been taken to the hospital."

He stared at me, then closed his eyes and tipped his head back, his eyes shut tight. Then he said, "What happened?" I told him. He opened his eyes and looked around like he was lost, then without another word, turned and ran. I called after him without effect.

I turned and looked at the lake. A light chop made it look like the waves were playing tag with the shore. Then Harry's boat flew around the corner of the island and shot toward the landing at Lyla's.

The beauty of the day belied its dreadful event. My cell vibrated in my pocket. Dave Messerli told me what I already expected, and I told him about my failure regarding the security system.

+ + +

I walked to the Smyth's cabin to tell Mae what had happened, then stepped outside to call Shorty Dvorak, but before I could dial, Tom Cooper and Otis, out for their morning stroll, appeared. Tom said, "I saw the sheriff and the EMTs. Can I do anything to help?"

"Could you please give me a lift to the mainland?"

"Certainly, Father. Follow me." We walked to his cabin, let Otis inside, then walked to his dock. I sat in the bow of Tom's skiff and said nothing.

+ + +

Tom dropped me at Lyla's. I thanked him and declined his offer to wait for me, knowing I would be in town for some time. Being the gentleman he was, he didn't pry, undoubtedly understanding a clergyman's need for confidentiality. Knowing how Tom felt about Penny, I didn't want to say anything to taint a future investigation.

I walked the four blocks to Bluestone Regional Health, checked in at the front desk, and was directed to the emergency room. Laurie Worth, a nurse at BRH I'd met at St. Aidan's breakfasts and fish fries, met me in the hallway. She greeted me and didn't have to ask why I was there. She led me to an examining room where John Smyth stood talking to a man with a stethoscope around his neck, a light blue shirt with a button-down collar, and tan chinos. Not wanting to interrupt the conversation, I stood in the doorway and waited.

John glanced at me out of the corner of his eye, turned, and motioned me in. The man I naturally assumed was the doctor on call when Penny was brought in was of medium height and build with closely-cropped dark hair. Harry Burns sat in a plastic chair, not listening.

John spoke softly. "Paul, this is Father MacManus from St. Aidan's. Father, this is Doctor Paul Kuh."

Doctor Kuh extended his hand. We shook and he said, "Nice to finally meet you, Father. Unfortunately, it is under these circumstances." He kept hold of my hand as his eyes shifted to Harry. Then he said, "I'll leave you gentlemen alone. Let me know

140

if there's anything you need." He let go of my hand and left, but not before resting his hand on Harry's shoulder.

I sighed and sat on the edge of the bed. John Smyth stood at attention. Harry sat, forearms on his knees, hands folded, eyes staring at nothing.

"Harry, I am so sorry," I said. He didn't move or speak. I let it alone, simply being there as he tried to process what had happened.

John broke the silence. "Harry, you've had a terrible shock. Would you like me to contact Everson's?"

Harry lifted his head a few inches and blinked. John looked at me, turned to Harry and said, "The funeral home."

Harry exhaled and nodded, still looking at nothing. John left to make the call. I sat with Harry and did what a good priest does.

Let the grief alone.

Chapter 39

St. Aidan's was filled to capacity Sunday morning. Small town news caries fast. Harry Burns was not in attendance.

"The Lord be with you," I announced to the overflowing crowd. Those who knew the drill responded with "And also with you."

"We like to think that nobody who comes here to worship is a visitor, just another soul looking for Christian fellowship and encouragement." I paused for a ten-count, then said, "The Requiem Mass for Penny Burns will take place here this Tuesday, July 5 at 10:00 a.m. You are all welcome to attend."

With that I recessed to the back of the nave where I met the white-robed Tom Cooper and Malcolm Macalester who were serving as assistants. Thelma, thankfully, introduced the correct processional hymn and sluggishly introduced "Father, We Praise Thee, Now the Night Is Over." All sang as they were able, and stopped singing when Thelma lost track and pulled out all the stops for one more superfluous stanza. Once she finished with a grand flourish, I faced the congregation and said, "Blessed be God: Father, Son, and Holy Spirit," to which the assembly responded from the printed order of worship, "And blessed be his kingdom, now and for ever. Amen."

The mass continued through the readings until the sermon. I crossed myself and mounted the pulpit not quite sure what would follow. When Jesus told his disciples "... do not worry about how or what you are to say; for it will be given you in that hour," I took Him at His word. I somehow managed to weave a message out of the readings for the day.

During the preparation for the eucharist, Ingrid Larssen accompanied herself on guitar to the hymn based on Psalm 91 that has become almost mandatory at Christian funerals of many denominations:

... And He will bear you up on eagles' wings,
Bear you on the breath of dawn,
Make you to shine like the sun,
And hold you in the palm of His hand ...

Ingrid sang several stanzas and choruses. Not a few congregation members wiped their eyes at the beauty of Ingrid's music in memory of Penny Burns.

The mass continued through the sacrament, the post-communion prayer, and blessing. Thelma led us out with the Common Doxology and so worship on this unusual day ended.

Chapter 40

The official cause of Penny's death was a severe brain injury exacerbated by hypothermia. At some point, she evidently fell backwards and hit her head on the corner of a storage shelf, evidenced by blood found at the scene. Her left shoulder was dislocated caused by her futile efforts to open the freezer door.

At 10:00 the following Monday night, Mae and I joined the other islanders sitting on our docks waiting for the annual Independence Day fireworks display sponsored by the Bluestone Fire Department. In Canada, this celebration would have taken place on the 1st of July, the date in 1867 when Nova Scotia and New Brunswick became united with the rest of what we now know as Canada.

The evening had cooled considerably, the summer crop of mosquitoes taking shelter in bushes and trees from the gusty wind. We sat wrapped in blankets, Mae's knitted hats on our heads to shelter us from the unseasonable chill.

The first rocket went up a few minutes after 10:00, followed by fifteen minutes of various pyrotechnics. After a short pause, the grand finale filled the sky with multi-colored showers, triple booms, and other explosions happening at the same time. Then silence followed by cheers and honking of car horns.

"Seems somehow wrong," said Mae. I knew she was thinking of Penny.

"Yes, but life does go on," I said, standing and reaching for Mae's hand. We headed back to the cabin, happy for America and sad for Harry Burns.

Chapter 41

After Penny's requiem mass the next day, I led the procession to Harry's dock. He carried the small wooden urn containing Penny's cremains, followed by the islanders who knew Penny or had been irritated by her: Tom Cooper, Millie TerHorst (surprisingly), John Smyth, Malcolm and Fiona Macalester, Mae, and assorted other islanders and townsfolk. I couldn't help thinking about how death, even the death of someone as annoying as Penny, caused people to ponder their own mortality.

For privacy's sake, Harry had asked me to accompany him out onto the lake, an unconventional graveside service, to be sure, but understandable. Harry helped me into his boat, handed me the simple box containing Penny's ashes, then stepped aboard, took his seat, turned the key, and the inboard motor came to life.

Tom Cooper had been drafted to untie the boat. Once that was accomplished, Harry backed slowly from the dock, then forward in a small semicircle into the light ripples where he cut the motor halfway between the island and the mainland.

"I guess this is it," said Harry, standing and turning to me. I stood also, handed Penny's remains to Harry and did my priestly duty, saying:

"In sure and certain hope of the resurrection to eternal life, through our Lord Jesus Christ, we commend to Almighty God our sister Penny, and we commit her ashes to their resting place; earth to earth, ashes to ashes, dust to dust. The Lord bless her and keep her, the Lord make his face to shine upon her and be gracious to her, the Lord lift up His countenance upon her and give her peace."

Harry took the lid off the simple urn, held it over the water, turned it upside down over the water, and watched Penny float away.

Fiona stood in full Highland dress, pipes at the ready four docks down from Harry's cabin. When he and I were back in our respective seats, the strains of "Flowers of the Forest" I'd requested she play imbued the air with its somber tune as we boated back slowly to the island, Harry and I both unashamedly weeping.

+ + +

Harry had requested no meal after the mass and subsequent interment. I'd counseled in favor, but finally went along with his wishes, knowing what a private man he was.

As Mae and I ate lunch by ourselves at home, she said, "Why were you crying when Fiona played that mournful tune? Was the music that forlorn?"

"Remember when we first heard her play it?"

"Yes."

"It's not the music that's so mournful. It's the words."

"What does it mean again, the song? Said Mae.

"It's a dirge lamenting the loss of a life."

"Flowers of the Forest" was played at my grandfather's funeral in Edinburgh when I was a wee lad. The old song referred to the men lost long ago at the defeat of the Scottish army at the Battle of Flodden in the fall of 1513, an example of how the past is never dead, it's not even past, as William Faulkner wrote in *Requiem for a Nun*. Less than a year after my grandfather's burying, my father, still mourning, emigrated with his family to Nova Scotia.

I swallowed and sang as best I was able:

I've seen the smiling of fortune beguiling,
I've tasted her pleasures and felt her decay;
Sweet is her blessing, and kind her caressing,
But now they are fled and fled far away.

We'll hear no more singing at our ewe-milking;
Women and children are heartless and sad;
Sighing and moaning on every green common—
The Flowers of the Forest are all scythed away.

+ + +

We decided to take our weekly island walk that Tuesday night instead of waiting for Wednesday. It seemed like a good idea considering the events of the day. We'd made our way to the other side of the island behind the stand of pines separating the cabins from the lake.

"Ironic, isn't it?" said Mae, who'd pulled me to a stop and turned toward the water.

"What do you mean?" I asked when she didn't follow her question with explanation. A light breeze rippled the lake and sang a light descant accompanying the waves lapping the shore.

"People come to the island to enjoy the warm Minnesota summer weather, and Penny dies in a freezer."

"Yes," I said. "Ironic indeed."

Chapter 42

Thursday morning promised a glorious summer day. Our inside door was open, allowing in the sweet smells of Tom Cooper's freshly-mown grass.

Mae and I had just finished clearing the table of our breakfast when we heard a gentle knock. I went to the door and said, "Harry. Won't you come in?"

He looked over my shoulder, saw Mae at the sink, and said, "I need to talk to you in private."

"Certainly," I said. "Shall we go to my office?"

He simply nodded, then stepped back to allow me out. I said a quick farewell to Mae and stepped out. Any effort to initiate a conversation with Harry on our way to the church was met with stony silence. I assumed he was still mourning and in shock, so I didn't press it.

Once we got to the office, I motioned for Harry to sit. I took the matching chair across from him.

"So," I said, letting Harry begin. I crossed my legs at the knee and folded my hands on my lap. Harry sat expressionless, straight as a Minnesota pine, his jeans worn but clean, his boots brushed, his T-shirt ironed, the last domestic happy task of Penny, I assumed.

"You noticed that she was different from most women," he said.

Not wanting to repeat the obvious, I simply said, "How do you mean?"

"Come on, Father. I never took you as naive." He shifted in his chair, hands on his knees. "Penny could rub people the wrong way."

Understatement, but I still needed to know what Harry really needed to unload. I needed background. "So, what brought you to Bluestone? I believe you arrived about the same time I did."

Harry leaned forward, then back. "I joined the Marines after high school, did my three-year tour, went to UM-Duluth for my Information Technology training, then got a job with a company based in California. Penny and I moved a lot. I could do my IT job from pretty much anywhere in the world as long as I had a secure internet connection."

I simply nodded my head in encouragement for him to continue.

"After I returned from my stint with the Marines, I made a promise that I've tried to keep all these years," said Harry. He swallowed, then said, "And I failed."

It's not uncommon to feel responsible for the tragic death of a spouse, but I had to ask, "You mentioned a promise."

Harry took a big breath and spoke. "I promised I'd take care of her."

"Of course," I said. "That's part of what marriage is."

He took another deep breath and said, "I promised our parents I'd take care of her."

"Of course," I said, and sat quietly.

Harry leaned over like he was trying to catch his breath after a marathon, then sat up and said, "You don't understand. When I said I'd promised our parents, I didn't mean my parents and her parents."

I blinked a few times, trying to interpret what Harry was telling me, then said, "I'm not sure I understand."

Harry looked over my shoulder, blinked, and said, "Penny was my sister."

Chapter 43

Taken aback does not do justice to how I reacted to that bombshell. I reacted in the classic way anyone does when gob smacked. I stared at Harry, furrowed my brow and whisper shouted, "What?"

"Everyone assumed we were married," he said.

"Yes," I said. "We did," trying to get my land legs under me.

"Penny was diagnosed with severe attention deficit hyperactivity disorder – ADHD – and obsessive-compulsive disorder – OCD – already in elementary school. She was six years younger than me. I was big for my age and spent a lot of time in the principal's office for fighting kids who made fun of her. Even got suspended once or twice. Our parents didn't believe in medication."

I sat as calmly as I could and let Harry talk, thinking of all the hidden woe people carried. After a time, he continued.

"I never married. I would have liked to have a real family, but I couldn't see any woman wanting to share a house with another woman of about the same age. And I made that promise to our parents. It was almost like a wedding vow, you know, only without the physical and emotional benefits. So I kept the promise all those years."

"And you never told anyone the truth until now?"

"No. I just let people think what they wanted, but I thought you should know."

Harry sat back and said no more. I counted to ten, then put both feet on the floor, leaned forward, and said, "Harry, it goes without saying that your story is safe with me. It took courage to tell me. You must feel, in some sad sense, liberated. How do you see yourself carrying on from here?"

"I can't think about it yet, but for now I'd like to stay here and fish. It's what I always did wherever we lived, sort of like therapy. Maybe in time I'll do some guiding on Bluestone and other area lakes. I'll also probably stay here through the winter and ice fish if that's allowed."

At the mention of fish, I thought of the freezer and inwardly winced.

"I have no problem with you staying through the winter, but we should check with the vestry. They have the final say on what happens on the island. Also, you should know the Bluestone police department will undoubtedly be contacting you. Penny obviously didn't lock herself into the freezer, and, as they say in law enforcement, the case is 'ongoing.'"

"They've already talked to me. Right now, I really don't care what they discover," he said. "Nothing an investigator will uncover will bring her back. It's all too surreal. Five days ago, she was here, and now she's not ..."

Harry stood and strode from my office without another word.

Chapter 44

Breakfasts and the Friday fish fry were cancelled all week in honor of Penny's demise and the kitchen being a "crime" scene. Dave Messerli had called several days ago to let me know an officer would be coming to begin the investigation of Penny Burns's death, so I was on the dock waiting when the Sherriff's boat pulled up to the communal dock at 8:00 Tuesday morning.

The boat glided to the dock, the officer hopped off and secured it to the dock cleats fore and aft with nylon rope, then approached me, held out her hand, saying, "Detective Ally Fletcher. You must be Father MacManus."

Since no one else was there dressed in a clergy shirt, I said, "Guilty as charged. How can I be of service to you?"

"I've been assigned to investigate the death of Penny Burns," said Officer Fletcher. "Could we find a private place to talk?"

"Yes, yes, of course, Detective. And please call me Angus."

I'm a priest and happily married, but I am also a man, albeit one approaching dilapidation, but Detective Fletcher was hard to ignore. She appeared to be in her late 20s or early 30s, her light brown hair with blonde highlights tied back in a pony tail and a face that would be at home in Hollywood with a figure to match. No makeup or other enhancements necessary. When she took off her mirrored aviator sunglasses her dark eyes held me like magnets.

Why did I tell her to call me Angus instead of Father MacManus? Shame on me.

I led her to my office, where I motioned for her to sit. She seemed supremely self-confident in the way some young people are. First, she pulled a small notebook out of her back pocket and one of the pens from her left breast pocket where she had hooked her aviators, then slid effortlessly into the chair like she'd taken etiquette lessons from Miss Manners.

I walked self-consciously around my desk and sat in my leather chair to put a professional distance between us. I asked if she'd like coffee. She declined.

I noted on the walk to the church she wore sturdy black shoes, dark blue pants and a matching blue short-sleeved shirt. Her badge was pinned on her belt. Patches below the epaulets on her shirt's shoulders identified her as a member of the Bluestone Police Department, established 1891.

I folded my hands, put my forearms on my desk, and said, "So. Penny Burns." Detective Fletcher turned slightly to face me, sat straight, her pad resting on her right leg, pen in her right hand, those magnetic eyes riveted to mine. I imagined if she ever questioned a male murder suspect, the case would be closed in five minutes.

"If you don't mind me asking, you seem quite young to have attained the rank of detective," I said, sweat trickling down my back and forehead, even in my air-conditioned office.

"Are you judging a book by its cover, Father?"

"No, no. Just an observation."

"Perhaps you've missed your calling," said Detective Fletcher, smiling a heart-melting smile. "It's not too late to apply to the academy. Detectives are always in demand."

"Even if I were interested in pursuing a career as a detective, which I'm not, I'm afraid that ship has sailed long ago."

"Back to your observation: I was fast-tracked due to the lack of detectives in smaller police forces in Minnesota. As a matter of fact, I am shared with a number of different municipalities, so the time spent on this case will be limited. Also, I don't look on age as a determining factor in anyone's work. After all, to paraphrase the Scripture, 'Skill can cover a multitude of experiences.'"

I thought of the differences in our ages, winked at Detective Fletcher, and said, "Touché."

"I understand from Sheriff Messerli that you found Mrs. Burns in the kitchen's walk-in freezer the morning of Saturday, July 2nd. Is that correct?"

"Yes," I said, thinking of Joe Friday on the old TV show *Dragnet* and his insistence on wanting "just the facts."

"I've spoken to Dennis O'Neill. I understand your church has security cameras aimed at various locations around the church including the kitchen. Is that correct?"

Again, "Yes."

"So you would have a record of what occurred in the kitchen the night of July 1 and morning of July 2."

"I should, but I don't," I said looking at my shoes and bowing my head.

"Why is that?"

I explained the security system and showed her my computer screen, then admitted the system had been disabled on the date in question because the office computer had somehow been turned off.

Ally made notes and thought for a moment before saying, "Can you account for your whereabouts the evening of July 1?"

"Am I a suspect?"

"Everyone's a suspect, Father."

"To answer your question, I was at our cabin with my wife, Mae."

"I'll check with your wife, although she's not your strongest alibi candidate. Can you think of anyone who would have wanted to harm Mrs. Burns?"

Instead of saying what I was thinking – or correct her use of Penny's title – I said, "Perhaps you should meet the island residents and come to your own conclusions."

Inspector Fletcher agreed. When I asked if I could be present while she questioned the church members since I was their spiritual advisor, she hesitantly agreed but insisted I remain silent during any interrogation. I gave the universal sign for silence, zipping my lip, turning the imaginary key and tossing it aside.

"Shall we visit each resident at their cottages or ask them to come here to the church office?" I asked.

"I'll start at their cabins," she said. "At this time, I see no need to intimidate people. If I need more information from a particular person, I will ask them to come to the station."

+ + +

"I can't say I'm surprised. She had it coming."

Millie TerHorst, in her typical gruff manner, stood in her doorway glaring at Ally and me, not inviting us in.

"Why do you say that?" said Ally.

"She was the typical home-wrecker, blatantly flirting with married men, and married herself! It wouldn't surprise me if she came on to you, Father." Millie glared at me, expecting a response which would not come.

+ + +

I suggested that we skip John and Belle Smyth since I was certain they had nothing to do with Penny's death, but Ally disagreed, saying they may not have caused the incident, but may have seen or heard something pertinent to the investigation.

John and Belle, as they often did, sat on their deck soaking up the morning sun. We came up behind them when I cleared my throat and bid them good morning, then said, "Allow me to introduce Detective Fletcher from the Bluestone police force," I said.

"Nice to see you again, Dr. Smyth," Ally said. I should have known their paths had probably crossed.

"And nice to see you, Ally," said John, standing and turning to face Officer Fletcher. "How is Ruger doing these days?"

"His training is progressing as expected. He should be fully certified by this fall."

Sensing I was confused and out of the loop, Ally said, "Ruger is a German Shepherd in training to be a Police Service Dog. Dr. Smyth actually led me to him last year."

"Ruger belonged to an acquaintance of mine who, due to his life circumstance, had to move to an apartment that did not allow pets. His loss was the department's gain." Belle remained seated, smiling over her shoulder.

"Dr. Smyth, I'm here investigating the death of Penny Burns. Were you at the fish fry on Friday, July 1?"

"Yes. Belle and I were both there. It's become a traditional weekly social gathering on the island."

"Did you see or hear anything in the kitchen that evening that would help me with my investigation?"

"We never go in the kitchen. Belle, as you know, has physical limitations. We left for our cabin after we ate."

+ + +

While we walked to Thelma Wadewitz's well-kept home, I told Detective Fletcher that Thelma was hard of hearing, so when Thelma answered the door, Ally introduced herself and the reason for the visit loudly. Thelma invited us in and told us to sit on her small loveseat while she sat in a rocker on the other side of her living room. I moved as far away from Ally Fletcher as possible, feeling like a shy schoolboy.

"Ms. Wadewitz, Father MacManus tells me that you may have been practicing organ after the fish fry on Friday evening, July 1. Is that true?" said Ally, leaning forward and speaking slowly and loudly.

"Oh, yes," said Thelma. "I always practice on Friday evenings since I'm already here for the fish fry. I always start by clearing the pipes." I remembered her arm composition. She smiled at Ally like the Cheshire cat.

"Were you in the kitchen that night?" said Ally.

"Yes, yes. Those pigeons are always roosting on the bell tower. They leave quite a mess, if you know what I mean."

Ally glanced at me, then back at Thelma and said loudly and slowly, "Were you in the church *kitchen* the night before Penny Burns was found in the freezer?"

Thelma knit her brow in thought, then said, "I don't quite remember ... Wait, yes, I may have been in the kitchen. My mouth gets terribly dry when I practice, you know, because I breath with my mouth open when I play, but I don't really remember if I went to the kitchen that night for a glass of water. I don't like to keep water at the organ because water spilled on the keys would be a catastrophe."

"Might you have been there to get a drink and noticed the freezer was unlocked and clicked the padlock shut?" Ally said slowly and emphatically.

"I ... I think I would remember that, but I just don't recall ..."

+ + +

We walked to Tom Cooper's cabin next. When he opened the door at Ally's knock and saw the fetching Detective Fletcher, he paused, smiled, then when he realized she was with the Bluestone police, took on an earnest expression.

"Tom, this is Detective Ally Fletcher. She is here with some questions regarding Penny's death."

He turned to me and said, "And you think I might have had something to do with it because she poisoned me?"

"Tell me about that," said Ally. Tom did, admitting it was probably an honest mistake, then told Ally he was actually still recovering at home from his trip to the ER and hadn't attended the fish fry that evening, a fact I confirmed.

Ally Fletcher reached into her pocket and handed a card to Tom. "Please call if you think of anything that might help with the investigation."

Tom looked at the card, then at Ally, and retreated into his cabin.

+ + +

Malcolm Macalester answered Detective Fletcher's knock and stepped out onto his porch. Fiona appeared and joined her husband. After my brief introductions, Malcolm said, "When can we get our kitchen back?"

"The investigation is still ongoing," said Ally, "but I imagine we'll have all the evidence we need soon. I'll let you know. Right now, I think you can plan on having your Friday fish fry next week."

"That should work," said Malcolm, turning to me. "Dennis promised to pick up the slack left by Harry's time off to mourn Penny's death. He said he'd keep fish in his home freezer until we could get back in the church kitchen."

Ally made a note in her small pad, then said, "You may have been the last people in the kitchen before Mrs. Burns was locked in the freezer." She didn't ask for a reply, but just looked at Malcolm and Fiona.

"I admit I did not like Penny," said Fiona, "but I did not lock her in the freezer. If I were out to do her harm, I'd have knocked her over the head with a Malcolm's rolling pin, which would have been faster and more effective."

"Penny could be a pest," said Malcolm, glancing at Fiona. "July 1 is our wedding anniversary and we were anxious to get home after the fry to have time to ourselves. Penny hung around like usual and volunteered to clean up the kitchen. We unfortunately agreed. The last thing I saw before we left was Penny loading dishes into the washer."

+ + +

After we left the Macalester's, I turned to Ally and said, "Would you like to talk to Harry Burns today?" I'd watched a few true murder mysteries on TV and knew the spouse was usually the first suspect.

"We talked to Mr. Burns last week."

"And?" I pressed.

"I can't comment, even to you, about an ongoing investigation, Father."

"Mm-mmm."

"I have several other cases in other counties for which I'm responsible and will take a good deal of my time," said Ally. She glanced at her watch, thanked me for my time, walked to the dock, boarded the department's boat, and left in a spray of lake.

Chapter 45

It seemed a number of people on the island had reason to harm Penny. But who did it and how did it happen? Was it on purpose or an unfortunate accident?

"What's your best guess on who locked Penny in the freezer?" said Mae on our now-traditional Wednesday evening stroll.

We kept walking, but I took time to think before saying, "I can't see Thelma, Tom, or Dennis being involved, although Thelma can't remember if she stopped in the kitchen for a drink of water that night. Fiona and Millie are at the top of my list, but it's not my place to accuse anyone. I'm content with letting the authorities handle it."

"But aren't you curious?"

"Of course, I am."

We walked on, almost three-quarters of the way around the island when I said to Mae, "Who is your top suspect?"

"Murder is always, if the crime dramas are to be believed, about love or money. Since I don't see anyone gaining financially from Penny's death – unless life insurance money is involved, and I'm sure the police have checked that angle with Harry – it must be love or its opposite. For that reason, Tom makes sense."

"From what I know of Tom Cooper, I can't see it," I said. "Of course, 'Who knows what evil lurks in the hearts of men…'" referencing an old radio show, *The Shadow*.

The Bluestone police boat pulled up to the main dock as Mae and I were about 50 meters away. Dave Messerli hopped out and tied off, then stood on the dock waiting for us. We stepped onto the dock, I shook his hand and said, "Sheriff Messerli! What brings you out on this fine evening?" like I didn't know.

He dropped my hand, turned to my wife and said, "I don't believe we've met. I'm Dave Messerli."

Mae reached to shake his hand and said, "I'm Angus's wife, Mae."

"Nice to meet you."

"So," I said, "is this business or pleasure?"

Messerli took off his Smokey Bear hat, turned his attention to me, and said, "First, it's always a pleasure to come to the island, but I'm afraid this visit is mainly business. I want you to know that Ally Fletcher is leaving the force. She's getting married and moving with her husband to Seattle."

I can't say I was surprised, but this seemed sudden. "When will this take place?" I said.

"She gave her two-week's notice three days ago. Since she was investigating Penny Burns's death, I thought you should know she thought the incident was a tragic accident and that the case should officially be closed. I agreed."

I stood there like a totem pole, not sure what to say. Mae broke the silence.

"So if we ever want to find out what happened, we're on our own?"

"Afraid so," said Officer Messerli. "With Detective Fletcher's departure, we just don't have enough personnel to follow up on what we do not consider a felony." He put his hat back on and said, 'But if any rodents are causing catastrophic issues, please don't hesitate to call."

"Well, thank you for informing me about Detective Fletcher," I said, getting the joke about the groundhog issue. Dave Messerli got back in his boat and headed back to the mainland.

Curses. Gob smacked again.

Chapter 46

Henry Martyn Robert, the 19th century U.S. Army officer who wrote the book on parliamentary procedure, spun in his grave the third Sunday of each month. This iteration of St. Aiden's vestry saw no need for order since the business of the parish normally took five minutes to accomplish, and gentlemen and lady's agreements kept things moving smoothly and quickly.

After I finished greeting the congregation after mass the third Sunday in July, I went to the meeting room to find the vestry waiting. I usually had to round them up to get the meeting underway. Something was up.

Today's meeting would not be smooth or quick. John Smyth sat looking at his hands, folded on the conference table. Millie TerHorst sat ramrod straight, staring daggers at me. Thelma smiled at Dennis, not hearing a thing.

Dennis O'Neill spoke as soon as I was seated. "Father, we need to talk about what happened to Penny."

I simply nodded and looked at Dennis. When he didn't continue, I said, "What is it you'd like to say?"

He cleared his throat and said, "As curious as I am, I don't think it appropriate to surmise how Penny came to be locked in the freezer, but ..."

He was fishing for information that I could not give, so I said, "As you all undoubtedly know by now, the Bluestone police investigated the incident. We can have theories and suspicions, but we should let the police do what they were trained to do." I did not mention that the case was closed.

John Smyth straightened and addressed Dennis. "Does the parish have any culpability? Will our insurance policy cover us if someone brings suit?"

"I'll look into it," said Dennis, "but who might sue us?"

I cleared my throat and said, "The only aggrieved person I could think of is Harry. I doubt he would take legal action anytime soon, but we don't know what he might do later." I thought for a moment and said, "It behooves all of us to keep our opinions on the matter to ourselves. Should someone be unjustly accused by any of us, the accused party could bring a personal suit for slander that would not necessarily involve the church as defendant, but would harm St. Aidan's reputation."

Millie's breath, rapid and audible, filled the space in the room while the rest of the vestry thought about the legal ramifications of Penny's death. Her lips were so tight they were turning blue. I could tell she was trying to hold it in, but she couldn't.

"I'm glad she's dead," she said. "The world is a better place with one less Penny Burns in it."

Everyone except Thelma – who sat in blissful silence – turned to Millie, then to me. I lifted my head and said, "Millie, surely you don't mean that."

"I most certainly do," she said, then stood, turned, and walked out of the meeting.

Was I the only one who noticed the tear rolling down her cheek?

Chapter 47

I'd learned from bitter experience that unpleasant confrontations are best dealt with early, so after the vestry meeting adjourned with no further business to enact, I made my way to Millie's cabin after stopping to tell Mae I would be late for lunch. She, also from experience, didn't ask why.

I tapped on Millie's door and waited. I tapped again, louder this time.

"What do you want?" Millie's voice came from behind me. She evidently had walked around the island, perhaps composing herself. Her curly hair had been disarrayed by the late morning wind that pressed her long plain cotton shift against her gaunt frame.

"We need to talk," I said, not so much referring to her outburst at the vestry meeting, but the reason behind it. I turned to her, she stood at the end of her walk and stared at me, a cigarette dangling from the corner of her mouth.

"Is she your first wife?" said Millie, nodding toward my cabin. As she nodded, a long ash fell from her cigarette. She took the white tube of tobacco from her mouth, dropped it in the grass next to her walk and ground it into the lawn.

"If you're referring to Mae, yes, she's my first and only."

Millie huffed, crossed her arms, and said, "Then you couldn't understand."

"What is it I couldn't understand?"

Millie shot her usual sour stare at me and said, "I suppose you should come in." She walked past me, opened her door, walked in, and left me to follow.

She stood by her dining table and said, "I suppose it would be unchristian of me to make you stand there like a cigar store Indian," motioning me to a plain wooden chair at her table. She sat opposite me, leaving me to wonder why she needed two since she had been supremely antisocial since we'd met.

164

We sat looking at each other, then I said, "You were obviously upset when you left the vestry."

The corners of her mouth dropped. She didn't take her eyes off mine, but her steely gaze suddenly changed.

"That chair you're sitting in," she said. I glanced down over my shoulder to look at the chair's nondescript legs.

"Yes?"

"Another man sat in that chair 40 years ago." Her eyes flicked from me to over my left shoulder. I remained silent. "Like you, he was a clergyman." She paused her story. I didn't respond.

"His name was Willard. He left the ministry."

"That must have been hard on him and his congregation," I said, wondering where this story was going.

"The church secretary also left with him," said Millie. I sat silently and then watched the lightbulb pop on in my thought bubble.

"Some said she was to blame, but as the saying goes, it takes two to tango," said Millie, looking down between her folded hands. Then she raised her head, glared at me, and said, "Now you know why I hated Penny Burns."

What little was left of my hair was standing on end. Millie TerHorst's explanation of herself and her past made me sad and angry at the same time.

After a considerable time of silence, I said, "Why do you keep this chair?"

She straightened her back, took a deep breath, and said, "To remind myself of my own stupidity."

Chapter 48

Mass on the last Sunday in July proved uneventful. Thelma did her usual thing, including playing the wrong recessional hymn. I did my thing, then everyone had coffee and went home to listen to the Twins beat Milwaukee on a walk-off homerun.

Monday Malcolm and Fiona provided the promised Half Burns Day breakfast – haggis, neeps (mashed turnips, also called 'swede') tatties (mashed potatoes), and Cullen skink, a thick fish soup. Malcolm also fixed scrambled eggs and hash browns for the less-gastronomically adventurous. Mae separated herself from me, deciding instead to sit with Thelma and Millie, leaving me alone until Dennis O'Neill pulled up a chair next to me and said in a low voice, "So, the saga of Penny is officially in our laps now."

"Afraid so," I said, drowning a mouthful of haggis with a large gulp of coffee.

Dennis continued sotto voce, "For what it's worth, I'm leery of Harry. It's always the spouse that did it on TV."

"Yes, well, I'm guessing we may never know what exactly happened. Even though the Bluestone police have officially closed the file, we should still keep our suspicions to ourselves. Gossip, as we know, spreads like a drop of motor oil on the lake."

"I'm not saying I'll be poking my nose into it," said Dennis, "but it sure would be nice to know what really happened."

"I agree, both about our noses and knowing."

+ + +

After breakfast I bid Mae farewell and trudged to my office. The phone rang before I could sit.

"Good morning. St. Aidan's-on-the-Lake, Father MacManus speaking. How may I help you?"

"That's what I wanted to ask you, Angus."

"Bob! To what do I owe this pleasure?" Another call from my bishop was a welcome distraction, especially since he'd encouraged me to be as informal with him as necessary.

"It's always a pleasure catching up with my priests," said the bishop. "I would have called sooner, but Jolene and I were out of the country on a pilgrimage to Canterbury."

"Lucky you," I said. "Someday Mae and I hope to do the same." I began to wonder if this was just a friendly call or if there was more to it.

"I've been told about the unexpected death in your parish, and I want to know how you're getting along. Death, as you well-know, is a fact of life for a priest, but one under suspicious circumstances can be particularly trying." I filled him in on Penny Burns's suspicious demise, the initial investigation, the departure of Ally Fletcher, Millie TerHorst's sad history, and the closure of the case.

"I've no interest in delving into the proceedings," said Bob. "That's not my purpose. I just want you to know I'm here as an ear or any other assistance you might need."

"Thank you for that," I said. "I'll ring you before we head to St. David's in September. Can you tell me anything about Bishop Moore?"

"Excellent, excellent man. You two will get on famously."

We chatted a bit longer about Texas, neeps, tatties, and haggis, then bid each other farewell.

Chapter 49

August weather in Minnesota can be horribly oppressive – temperatures in the upper 90s with humidity levels to match. Mae and I still took our weekly Wednesday walks around the island while all the island's cabin's doors and windows were shut, air conditioners humming.

We dressed as skimpily as possible. I still stuck to long pants, but deserted a clergy shirt for my old Grateful Dead T-shirt. I always thought the name of the band should have had more of a Christian emphasis than it did, relating it to the resurrection of the body and the life everlasting we confessed in the creed every Sunday. Mae wore walking shorts, a thin white sleeveless top, and sandals while I wore an old pair of sneakers, sans socks.

"When are you thinking you'll retire?" said Mae.

The subject didn't come up often, but as I was approaching the age – and had been a card-carrying member of AARP since arriving in Minnesota – I supposed thinking about it sooner rather than later for my super-organized wife would be important.

"Why do you ask?" I said. Answering a question with another question is part of my tool kit.

"Since we are not paying rent or a mortgage here, I've been putting away what we would be spending for housing in a dedicated account. Your salaries at St. Aidan's and St. David's are well-above the national average for Episcopal clergy of your experience level. If we continue that practice for five years, we should be financially fine should you decide to retire then."

Five years. I've never really thought much about it, but now Mae is asking me to do it.

Five years. Half a decade. I'd only be 60.

When I did think about retirement, I knew other clergy who supplied pulpits on almost a weekly basis. I didn't think I'd want to do that. Nearly impossible to know a congregation and its people.

"You know, of course, how to make God laugh," I said.

"Yes, yes; tell Him your plans."

"So let's not force Him into convulsive giggling."

Chapter 50

I'd contacted who I considered to be "the usual suspects" after mass the last Sunday in August – I had to track Harry down since he didn't attend – and asked them to meet me in the conference room after breakfast the following day. The summer was quickly coming to its end and I was still seeking closure on what happened to Penny.

Millie TerHorst arrived early, as was her custom. Her demeanor had changed somewhat after she unburdened herself to me. This morning I almost detected the vague hint of a smile, or at least the absence of a scowl.

Thelma came in a minute after Millie. She carried her antique briefcase packed with music, some of which was sticking out of the sides of the case. When she plopped it heavily on the conference table, it sprung open and its contents spilled onto the floor.

"Let me help you," I said, bending down on one knee to retrieve her jumble of music, pencils, paper clips, and sticky notes, among which I found my letter opener and Montblanc pen.

"Ah! So that's where they went!" I said, standing and holding them up for Thelma to see before putting them in my shirt pocket.

She looked at me innocently and said, "Oh, are those yours? I think I borrowed them to open some mail from music publishers that came to the church and note any music I'd want to buy and forgot to return them. I hope you don't mind."

Before I could respond, Tom and Dennis entered the room right on time, and Harry a minute after. By now Thelma had stuffed her music back in her briefcase and snapped it shut, smiling like an innocent child. Millie sat in her usual chair, surprisingly patient.

Malcolm and Fiona were the last to arrive, having sufficiently tidied the kitchen and themselves.

Once everyone was settled, I sat at the head of the table and began the meeting saying, "Thank you all for coming this morning. I know we all have much to do in the next weeks after Labor Day, but I thank you for humoring me. Like our departed sister Penny, I am a bit OCD, heavy on the obsessive."

"Like me and that bloody door," said Dennis, which got a chuckle going in the room.

"Before leaving her post here for Seattle, Detective Fletcher was very helpful in attempting to solve the riddle of how Penny was locked in the freezer. As a matter of fact, she cleared all of you, so while what I have to say is not an official inquiry into the case, I'd like you to hear me out anyway."

Everyone was silent, probably thinking they were about to be accused regardless of Detective Fletcher's investigation.

"Understand these are only theories, but sometimes talking a thing through can find truth, or lead to the truth, so please don't take my theories as attacks on you. Consider this more of a fishing expedition, more of an 'is it possible' kind of thing. And please, no comments until I'm finished."

Everyone sat stone still, probably thinking I was about to crack the case and they were the one on whom the hammer would fall.

"First of all, Dennis. It it possible that, as the exemplary warden we all know you to be, you checked the building the Friday evening before Penny was discovered in the freezer, saw the lock was hanging loose, and simply clicked it back in place?"

He looked like he was about to speak in his defense, but before he could talk, I raised my hand palm out, and continued:

"And Thelma, is it possible you came to the kitchen after your post-fish fry practice for a drink of water, and, as you've said, cannot remember doing it or closing the lock?"

She didn't look like she'd been listening.

"And Tom. Knowing you as I do, I can't see any possible connection to why you would have been in the kitchen that evening, but you did have a grievance against Penny." Everyone on the island and most of the town had heard of Tom's near-death experience. I didn't mention the prolonged grief over the loss of his wife and the effect that may have had on him. He nodded and looked at his hands, folded on the table.

"And Millie, is it possible you stopped in the ladies' room after the meal, and being security conscious, came back to check the kitchen, noticed the freezer was unlocked, and locked it without knowing if anyone was inside?"

Millie stared at me and shook her head.

"Fiona and Malcolm, is it possible you were in the kitchen and didn't know Penny was in the freezer when you, being the thorough chefs you are, closed the lock?"

Harry, who appeared to be in a world apart during my hypothesizing, slowly stood and said, "Excuse me," then walked out of the room. Assuming he had to use the restroom and would be back soon, the rest of the assembled – except Thelma, who was blissfully unaware of the proceedings – took turns shooting holes in my theories.

In ten minutes, Harry had not returned and nobody confessed to locking Penny in the freezer, so my unofficial inquiry came to an end and we parted on relatively friendly terms. My fishing expedition ended with nary a bite, as I expected.

I stopped in the men's room on my way back to my office. Harry wasn't there. On my way back to our cabin, I saw Harry's boat on the lake, headed for the other side of the island and into the vast expanse of Bluestone Lake.

Chapter 51

The last fish fry of the season was scheduled for the second Friday in September. Most Minnesotans, I'd learned, closed up their cabins Labor Day weekend. I'd heard rumblings the last week of August of people prepping for moves to yonder places, which was all the talk at the Friday feasts as summer's end approached.

John and Belle Smyth, Millie TerHorst, and Malcolm and Fiona Macalester would be joining me at St. David's; Dennis and Trudy O'Neill were headed to one of their children in California after buttoning up the kirk for the winter; Tom Cooper would be staying at his condo in Minneapolis until spring; Thelma Wadewitz was off to spend the winter with her "little sister" in Florida, her sister being only three years younger.

I planned a "hail and farewell" message for the third Sunday of September, which would be the last mass at St. Aidan's until next April.

After the passing of the peace – which took a goodly amount of time because everyone shook hands with everyone else and hugged and chitchatted, except Millie, who did not wander the sanctuary and only shook hands when someone offered – I unwound myself from my flock, stood by the front pew, finally got them all seated, and said, "As you may or may not know, today's mass is the last of the summer here at St. Aidan's. Many of you will be moving on to your winter homes while some of you are staying nearby to keep the home fires burning. For those of you staying, I pray for you peace of mind and a mild winter. For those of you moving to St. David's with Mae and me or to other warm climes, I pray for you safe travels and the anticipation of seeing old friends and meeting new."

We continued with Holy Communion, always a most sacred time for a priest. Once all had communed, I blessed the congregation and Thelma led us out with the Common Doxology:

Praise God, from whom all blessings flow;
Praise Him, all creatures here below;
Praise Him above, ye heavenly host;
Praise Father, Son, and Holy Ghost.

Then after a final rousing "Amen," she improvised on the well-known song by Roy Rogers and Dale Evans that does not appear in our hymnal: "Happy Trails to You, Until We Meet Again."

Cranmer hopped off Belle Smyth's lap and, almost presciently, found Dennis and rubbed against his shin.

Chapter 52

Our supper that Sunday night consisted of various leftovers and whatever other odds and ends we could find in our kitchen, knowing our time on Bluestone was coming to an end for the half-year.

"You certainly are restrained this evening," said Mae. I nibbled on a Ritz cracker spread with cream cheese and pepper jelly, realizing I hadn't said a word for over five minutes, a straight-up record for a preacher.

Knowing her mind was on the impending trip south and the necessary plans attached, I fibbed. "Sorry. Guess I'm just trying to reflect on the summer and imagine what the winter in Texas will be like." I was not ready to share my frustration with the whole on-going Penny Burns situation.

"What are your plans for tomorrow?" said Mae.

"I should probably go to my office and decide what needs to be packed," a task I was dreading.

"If you'd like my advice, pack light, and remember that the information in most of your theological volumes is available somewhere on the internet."

"But is the internet even available there?" I joked. "I've heard Texans are an independent lot."

She smirked, gave me "the look," and said, "It's not called the *'World-Wide-Web'* for nothing."

+ + +

My attempt at sleep that night was interrupted by dreams of fish, padlocks, bagpipes, and law enforcement officials. At 3:30 I got up as quietly as I could so as not to disturb Mae, who always slept the sleep of the dead anyway.

After a stop in the loo, I padded to the living room. The early-autumn temperature wasn't warm enough to start the AC nor cool enough to kick in the heater, so I stepped out for some fresh air, hoping I could get back to bed and recoup at least a few hours' sleep.

A gibbous moon gave enough light that a movement on the lake caught my eye. A boat glided silently toward the mainland, obviously powered by an electric trolling motor. I watched until it pulled up at Lyla's dock, but without my spectacles I couldn't see who might be out in the middle of the night.

I went back inside and made coffee, knowing sleep would be futile.

+ + +

By 5:00 I'd finished the rest of the coffee and started a fresh pot just as Mae appeared in her old summer nightgown.

"You sure are up early," she said.

"So are you," I said.

"Lots to do. The early bird and all that," she said, yawning.

"Coffee's brewing for you. I may as well get to it as well," I said, heading for the shower. Once properly laved and shaved, I got dressed and hugged Mae on my way out.

"Wait," she said. "I'll make you breakfast. Not much left except toast and instant oatmeal."

"No need," I said. "I'll just be back around 10:00 for an early lunch, if that's OK with you, then back at it this afternoon packing up the office."

"Doesn't it seem like we only arrived last week and now it's time to be heading south?" said Mae.

I did a quick mental check on everything that had transpired over the summer and hesitantly agreed with a simple nod. Too early in the morning for that discussion, so I gave Mae a shoulder hug and headed to the church.

+ + +

The deciduous trees on the island had begun their annual change from green to bursts of yellow and red, the height of which would not occur until October. I would have to get used to not experiencing the total change of seasons, although I had not a clue what fall and winter would be like in Texas other than much more temperate than Nova Scotia or Minnesota.

I entered the church by the front door, happy that my appeal to keep the doors unlocked as tradition dictated was accepted by the vestry, much to Millie's dismay. I processed to the altar rail, knelt, and prayed for guidance. Then, in full confidence of God's direction, stood and headed to my office.

I flipped on the light switch inside the office door and took a minute to look at the shelves behind the desk. I hated to think of the treasured volumes that, by their simple presence, fed my soul – even though the knowledge and wisdom in most hadn't been solicited for years – would stay here, waiting for my return like a faithful dog.

"As usual, Mae is right," I thought. "The internet is way lighter than lugging boxes of books."

I sighed, then walked around my desk and sat in that luxurious chair, wondering what furnishings awaited at St. David's. Rolling up to the desk and computer, I saw an envelope addressed to me propped against the laptop's screen.

"Probably a good-bye message from someone," I thought, slicing it open with my recovered letter opener. I pulled the paper from the envelope and read the handwritten note:

Father MacManus,

You asked interesting questions at your "fishing expedition," Sorry I couldn't stay, so I'll tell you what you would have said to me.

Is it possible you are what is known as a 'quiet drunk?'

Is it possible you sat alone at the fish fries, not because you are necessarily introverted, but because you needed to keep an eye on Penny but didn't want people to smell the alcohol on your breath?

Is it possible your drinking problem you use as an anesthetic and Penny's hounding you to get help finally caused a meltdown?

Is it possible when you left the fish fry that night you went home and drank too much?

Is it possible you finally decided you'd had enough of your 'wife' (I know you would not have revealed my real relationship to Penny to the others). Then, in your inebriated state, came back to the church intending to finally confront her. You deleted your entrance captured on the security system camera, then powered off your computer including the kitchen camera, saw Penny in the kitchen, pushed her into the freezer, and as immature as it sounds, locked her in to scare her?

Is it possible you then went back to your cabin to let her 'chill' for a while, intending to return later and let her out?

Is it possible you took a nap on your couch but had drunk so many shooters in an effort to numb yourself from the years of keeping that promise to your parents, that you passed out until the next morning when you came to, not remembering what happened the night before?

Please tell the powers-that-be on the island that I will not renew my lease next summer.

Harry Burns

+ + +

While Harry's letter was not an outright confession and would undoubtedly not hold up as evidence in court, I invoked for myself the confidentiality of the confessional and decided that since the Bluestone police had essentially shelved the case, I would not be the one to reopen it. Harry Burns would suffer the rest of his life. I tore his letter into shreds and tossed it into the recycling bin, then packed my Montblanc, letter opener, and a few other necessities into my briefcase.

Chapter 53

The third Thursday in September, all our belongings that would fit in our vehicle were packed and transported to the mainland on Shorty Dvorak's pontoon. He waited as we walked to Fischer Ford and returned with our van, which he graciously helped us pack.

Somewhere near Des Moines, Mae said from her shotgun seat, "Are you intentionally ignoring me?" She didn't mention that for a good part of the four-plus hour drive she'd been napping. We'd left Bluestone around 10:00 a.m., stopped for lunch at a Subway in Rochester, then headed down I-35.

I took my right hand off the steering wheel, reached over, took her hand and said, "Sorry. Just not very talkative today. I guess the adrenaline of the past week has worn off." I'd decided that Harry's letter would have to be a burden I would bear.

Mae had charted our trip to St. David's, making reservations at a Days Inn in a suburb of Kansas City. We arrived at 6:00 p.m., checked in, and dined on famous KC Barbecue at the adjacent restaurant. Fully sated, we returned to our lodging, slept and snored like hibernating bears, got up at 5:00 a.m., had the complimentary breakfast of artificial scrambled eggs, biscuits and gravy, juice and coffee, then headed south to become "Winter Texans" and experience the surprises, scandals, revelations, challenges, discoveries, and above all, the people at St. David's.

No matter where we hang our hats and coats,
No matter if we settle near or far;
Whether we drive pickups, vans, or boats
Be sure to know that's where God's people are.

RECIPES

Deep-fried Freshwater Fish

Ingredients

- Fish filets of your choosing (panfish, perch, walleye preferred)
- Milk
- Flour, seasoned with salt and pepper
- Crushed crackers (saltines or Ritz)

Drench fish filets in flour, then milk, then crackers. Drop one-by-one in hot oil – don't crowd. Remove from oil when they float to the surface. Drain on paper towels. Serve with tartar sauce or sandwich spread.

Haggis

Ingredients

- ½ tablespoon butter
- 1 onion
- ½ teaspoon ground black pepper
- ¾ teaspoon ground coriander
- ¾ teaspoon nutmeg
- 1 teaspoon allspice
- ½ teaspoon dried thyme or fresh, slightly chopped if fresh
- ¼ teaspoon cinnamon
- 1 lb ground lamb
- ½ lb chicken livers
- 1 cup stock
- 4 oz pinhead oatmeal

Directions

1.   Preheat the oven to 350F.
2.   Warm the butter in a pan. Finely dice the onion and cook over a medium heat in the butter until softened, about 5 minutes.
3.   Meanwhile, take any fatty or tough pieces off the chicken livers and roughly chop.
4.   Add the various spices and thyme to the onion and cook a minute then add the lamb and chicken livers.
5.   Brown the meat, then once it is all cooked, add the stock and cover. Allow to simmer for around 20 minutes.
6.   Next, add the oatmeal; mix well and transfer to an oven dish (unless you started with a dish that can transfer).
7.   Cover the dish and put in the oven for 30 minutes.
8.   Remove the lid and cook another 10 minutes.
9.   Serve with mashed potatoes and mashed rutabaga/swede.

Neeps and Tatties

Ingredients

- 8 large baking potatoes, washed, peel left on and cut into 1½ inch chunks
- 6 tbsp light olive or sunflower oil
- 1 swede (rutabaga) weighing about 1½ pounds, peeled and roughly chopped
- 3 tablespoons butter, plus extra for serving

Directions

- STEP 1

  The day before you want to serve, preheat the oven to 375 degrees. Put the potatoes into a pan of lightly salted water, return to the boil and cook for 5 minutes. Drain the potatoes, put them back into the pan and place it back on the heat for a couple of minutes to dry out.

- STEP 2

  Meanwhile, pour the oil into a large roasting pan (you may have to use two) and heat it in the oven until smoking hot. Now stir the potatoes into the hot oil and return to the oven to roast, turning occasionally, for 55 minutes.

- STEP 3

  Cook the swede in boiling salted water for 50-55 minutes, or until very soft. Drain and add to the roasted potatoes. Roughly mash everything together, keeping quite chunky, then cool, cover and keep in a cool place.

- STEP 4

  To serve, preheat the oven to 350 . Uncover the potatoes and swede, dot with the butter and put in the oven to reheat for 25-30 minutes, stirring now and again until piping hot. Serve with lots of butter.

Cullen skink

Ingredients

- 2½ cups milk
- 1/4 cup parsley sprigs, leaves and stalks separated, more leaves for garnish
- 1 bay leaf
- 1 pound smoked haddock fillet, preferably not dried
- 4 tablespoons unsalted butter
- 1 medium onion, finely chopped
- 1 to 1½ cups store-bought or homemade mashed potato
- Kosher salt, to taste
- Freshly ground black pepper, to taste
- Crusty bread, for serving, optional

Directions

1. Gather the ingredients.
2. Put the milk, parsley stalks, bay leaf, and the whole piece of haddock into a large saucepan.
3. Finely chop the parsley leaves. Set aside.
4. Bring the milk to a gentle boil over medium heat. Lower the heat to low simmer, about 3 minutes.
5. Remove the pan from the heat. Set aside for 5 minutes so the herbs and haddock infuse their flavors into the milk.
6. Remove the haddock from the milk with a slotted spatula. Set aside.
7. Strain the liquid through a fine mesh strainer. Discard the herbs.
8. In another large saucepan over medium-low heat, add the butter and the onion. Cook gently until the butter melts and

the onions become translucent, about 5 minutes. Be careful not to burn the onion.

9. Add the infused milk and the potato to the onion-butter mixture. Stir until the potatoes dissolve and the soup thickens slightly.

10. Flake the smoked haddock into bite-size chunks, discarding any bones. Add to the soup.

11. Lower the heat to a gentle simmer. Add the chopped parsley and cook until the haddock is warmed through, about 5 minutes. Don't over-stir, because the fish chunks might disintegrate.

12. Season to taste with salt and pepper. Be careful with the salt, as the fish will impart quite a salty flavor all on its own.

13. Garnish the soup with the reserved parsley leaves and more freshly ground black pepper. Serve with crusty bread, if desired.

Other books by Larry Finke

Smiling Out Loud
Smiling Out Loud Again
Said Sid
Safe at Home
Close Call
Available on Amazom.com

I Wish You Christmas
Available on Lulu.com